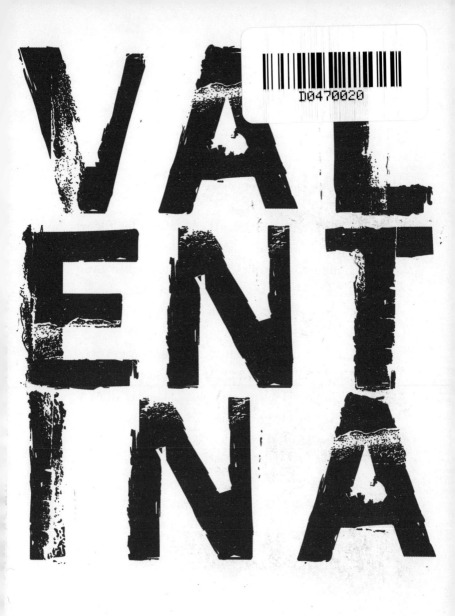

VALENTINA

about the author

Kevin Mc Dermott lives in Dublin with his funny, smart wife, Mary; their daughter, Sinéad (Roe), and the family cat, Brunelleschi. His son Eoghan lives in London and his daughter Aoife in Cardiff. Kevin works in teacher education and is editor of *Teaching English* magazine.

Kevin was a swot in school and went on to study English and Old and Middle English in college. He loved college and keeps going back. He has an MA in English Language Studies, an MLitt in English Literature and a PhD in Education.

He is always scribbling. The idea for *Valentina* came from reading one of James Lovelock's books on climate change. He was so taken with Lovelock's ideas that he a) went to Italy for three months and wrote the novel and b) moved to a new house way above sea level. He'd love to see a film version of *Valentina* with Tom Waits providing the soundtrack.

Kevin McDermott is the author of *A Master of the Sultan* (1997) and *Watching Angels* (2000).

VALENTINA

KEVIN McDERMOTT

VALENTINA
Published 2012
by Little Island
7 Kenilworth Park
Dublin 6W
Ireland

www.littleisland.ie

ISBN 978-1-908195-20-3

Cover design and layout by Paul Woods / www.paulthedesigner.ie

Printed in Poland by Drukarnia Skleniarz.

Little Island received financial assistance from
The Arts Council (An Chomhairle Ealaíon), Dublin, Ireland.

10 9 8 7 6 5 4 3 2

For M. A. E. S.
as always

And for my editors, Siobhán Parkinson
and Elaina O' Neill, with thanks

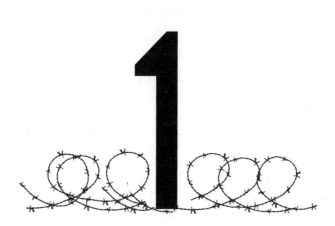

Everything changed when the ice cap collapsed and the number of immigrants trying to get on board our island ran into millions. I'll tell you a bit more about that as we go along. Also, it was the summer of the feral boy. That's what Dad called him. I had to look the word up in a dictionary. Feral: wild, savage. I'll tell you about him now.

The boy in question was named Damian and his family were new to the Citadel. Apparently they were chieftains of the Tribe a zillion years back, and had vast tracts of land in the Amber Zone. That was fine until Damian and his mother were snatched by the AOT (that's the Army of the Tribe, which sounds all legal and official, but isn't) and held until a ransom was paid. After that, they petitioned the council and were allowed to live in the Citadel, having paid a ridiculous amount of money for the privilege.

And then my mum and I were invited over to lunch. We're the first family in the Citadel. We socialise with maybe the next fifteen families. The new family was number 280 out of 300 – way down the league. That's why it was a big deal for us to visit them.

You have to pay to live in the Citadel. There are families from our Tribe who have lived here from the time of the Arctic, but there are also families from all over the globe. I mean all over. Race and colour don't matter in the Citadel. If you have the means you can apply, which doesn't mean you get a place, but if you do then you have to promise to live by the Book. That's the Book of Rules. If you don't abide by the Book, you're expelled.

I'd say Damian's parents paid a lot of money to the council to have us visit. I'm not sure about that, but I suspect that's what happened. Anyway, that's how I met Damian.

Poor old Damo – not so much the devil-child his name suggests as a big awkward dog who knocks over all the ornaments in the house. Except he wasn't big and he didn't actually knock things over, but his manners were primitive. You could see he just wanted to wolf down all the food laid out for the buffet lunch. Don't know if that's what comes of being brought up in the Amber Zone or if it was a result of being held in captivity. His mother was on edge, pleading with him with her big teary eyes to behave in front of the president's wife and daughter. I smiled at him and he looked back with those big, innocent, wary eyes.

He and I went out to the garden after lunch. He breathed a sigh of relief once he felt the fresh air on his face. We walked around the perimeter of the garden and then sat in the pergola and watched the water of the fountain. I couldn't get a word out of him. He was shy, certainly, but it was more than that. I don't think he thought much of me, which was a novelty, given that I was accustomed to all kinds of people falling over themselves trying to please me. It's not good for a girl, that, but you can get very used to it.

The family's cat came and sat on my lap but when Damian rubbed his hand on her fur, she stiffened, arched her back and hissed at him. He put his face down to hers and hissed back with such ferocity that the cat jumped from my lap and fled. Damian laughed.

'Where did you learn to do that?' I asked.

'In the real world, you learn all kinds of stuff.'

'You were in the Badlands?'

His face clouded over when I asked that and he began to study the thread in his trousers as if it was the most important thing in the world.

'Did I say something wrong?'

No response, just running his finger round and round the fabric of his trousers. He got up and started to walk back to the house.

'You can't just walk away.'

'Come back next week,' he said, without looking back.

'Well,' my mother asked on the way home, 'how did you get on with the found boy?'

'Fine.'

My mother hated it when I said 'fine' – so guess what? I said it all the time.

She ignored the provocation. 'His parents want you to help educate him.'

'You mean I'll have to go back?' I tried to look disgusted.

'If your father allows it.'

I turned away and stared out the window. I didn't much like my mother. She was all for doing everything by the Book. She said I had to set an example because we were the first family. When I asked her anything – anything important – she fobbed me off: 'You needn't concern yourself with that' or 'Things are better like this' or 'Things are never that simple' or 'You must trust your father's judgement.' Once I screamed at her, 'Do you ever think for yourself?' and she replied in that infuriatingly calm way of hers, 'There's far too much importance given to personal opinion, Valentina. Better to have faith than opinions.'

She was really annoying, my mother, but mostly I hated her because she hadn't tried hard enough to stop my brother Mattie from leaving. Mattie, my best friend, who told me stories at night, who included me in the elaborate games he devised with his friends, who laughed at my jokes. I missed him.

I don't like waking up, as a general rule. I'm happier in the dream world. Weird, isn't it – dreaming? It's you in your dreams and you know it's you, but then everything else is not quite right, like living in a house that's tilted on its side so when you walk you feel giddy and light-headed. And the world is so bright, so vivid. In dreams there's more of everything: more fear, more happiness, more monkeys, more dead people, more rainbows, more lakes, more fish – just more. And I'm more me in my dreams, more myself, more true to myself, more who I want to be. I don't much like the awake me, I suppose.

But the thing is that on the morning I was due to visit Damian again, I woke up no problem. I wanted to be awake and in this world. Now that was something new, something interesting, something different. So, I was awake and in my dressing gown, stroking Eccles (my cat) and thinking about what I was going to wear when Francesca, our maid, came with my breakfast tray.

There's no big deal about having a maid. Everyone in the Citadel has one, and a cook and a gardener and a driver and guards. That's one of the rules in the Book. You keep servants so everything will be perfect. And your servants have to be perfect, have to know all the rules, have to speak at least two languages fluently. My father has a theory that civilisation, our way of life, will only survive if the servants are more fanatical than the leaders in wanting to preserve it. His answer to 'Who will guard the guardians?' is always the same: the servants. So we have servants. And yes, Francesca, who speaks French, Italian and Russian, brings breakfast to my room every morning. You could call it being spoilt, or you could call it being bloody imprisoned.

Of course it is posh, my room. In fact, it isn't a room at all – it is my own private suite. Sounds better than the reality, especially back then. In reality, I slept there and hid there, but it was cleaned twice a day so it never felt like my room, my personal space, my own private refuge from the world. No, it was just a place I wasn't allowed to mess up or change. I envied people of my age their pigsty rooms. I wanted to paint the walls black and daub slogans in white – 'Down with slavery', 'Boys suck', that sort of thing – but Mother was having none of it. You've guessed it – the Book of Rules didn't allow for the defacement of beautiful things by ill-disciplined youth, blah, blah, blah.

When I had gone to visit family 280 with my mother we'd had an armed escort of two black limousines. Now it was just one car with the driver, Eddie, and my personal guard, Geraldine, who was nice enough if she wasn't too scared to talk to me. Why would she be scared? Because I had a reputation. I had previous.

The guard before her, Dimitri, freaked me out, see. He was just there all the time, looking at me, saying nothing, staring at me with these weird eyes. Too pervy by half. It was like being stalked by a paedo. (That's the kind of word to make my mother mad: twitch of her eyebrow, sharp intake of breath, faint frown in her creaseless forehead.) Anyway, I complained to my father that Dimitri was looking at me in a way I found 'sexually threatening'.

My father doesn't give much away about anything. I know he is called 'The Inscrutable' (and probably all kinds of other names that I never get to hear). He didn't fly off the handle or threaten to kill Dimitri or any of the things I imagine normal fathers would do and say if their precious fourteen-year-old daughter told them about being stalked by a perv. I think he nodded twice and then asked about school in this polite, remote way he had of communicating with me as if I was some random girl who wandered into the house and he knew he knew her but couldn't quite place who she was.

But, hey presto, that was the end of dear old pervy Dimitri. Sent off to the Badlands or some place beyond the borders of the State of Free Citizens. Which proves that Dad might act as if he is a giant sleeping bullfrog at the centre of the pond, but you should never underestimate him.

So where was I? Oh yes, Geraldine. That morning, on the journey to Damian's, I wanted to talk to Geraldine, tell her how excited I felt, how the sun in the sky was not the fearful thing that everyone dreaded, but the source of life. I wanted to tell her that it felt good to be alive and part of the world. I wanted to ask her if a boy had ever made her feel like I felt, even though I hardly knew him.

'Good morning, Geraldine,' I said.

'Good morning, Miss Valentina,' she answered, all stiff and starchy, with a suspicious, worried look on her face. I could tell she was thinking to herself, This little bitch is up to something, but I'm not going to get myself sent off to the Badlands. When I saw the way she looked at me, I just dropped it and sat looking out the window, wondering if I was doomed to be met with suspicion for evermore. I was no longer expecting a whole lot from my visit to Damian.

It wasn't much fun at first, me and Damian sitting in the garden saying nothing with Geraldine hovering on the margins and Damian's mother poking her head out a hundred times to see if we were all right.

It was warm. Well, it was always warm, but not so hot that everything was tinder-dry and waiting to combust. No, that's other places: places that begin with S. S for sizzle. Sizzling Sardinia. Sizzling Sicily. Sizzling Southern Spain. Sizzling Sahara. Sizzling South Africa. But not here. We're cool. We're temperate. We're safe. A little lifeboat island where it's possible to live in comfort and grow food and live 'like civilised human beings', as my father is so fond of saying.

That's what the Book of Rules is about, making sure people understand what it means to live in 'a civilised society'. The Elite, all 300 families, are the wealthiest and the most civilised. I get tired of being told what a blessing it is to live in our island paradise, or that part of paradise that is controlled by the Council, while half the world burns or is submerged under flood waters.

Somehow, in order to contribute to the continuation of our civilisation, I had to sit there with the silent devil-child. Why did I ever want to leave the dream world to sit with this infuriating boy?

And then, as if he was reading my thoughts, he said, 'Come to my room. I want to show you something.'

His room was almost a carbon copy of mine, but not as stylish, naturally, or as big.

Damian locked the door. Geraldine banged on it but I told her it was fine. Poor Geraldine. There was no way she was supposed to leave me on my own with anyone, never mind in a locked room with a boy I hardly knew. In terms of dereliction of duty, this was off the scale – any scale: Richter, Fahrenheit.

'I'll call you if I need you,' I added.

'Miss Valentina, this is not agreed procedure.'

'Chill, Geraldine, it's fine,' I said, looking at Damian. He smiled. It was the first time I'd seen that smile and it changed him. Before I knew it I was smiling back at him and I knew it would be OK.

'I'm right here if you need me, Miss.'

'Thank you,' I said. 'And I won't tell my father about this, OK?' That was nasty, I know. I can be a bitch when I want to be.

And then I got back to enjoying doing what passes for normal with most kids – hanging out with a friend.

'Well, come on, then,' I said. 'I'm waiting. You're going to educate me on the Badlands, right?'

'Patience,' he said, and went and sat at his desk. He started drawing on a large sketch pad. I went and stood by his shoulder. He drew a rough map of the island and began dividing it into sections.

It wasn't a very good drawing. And the last thing I needed was a geography lesson. Did he think the daughter of the president didn't know the island was divided? Did he think I wasn't aware of the troubles beyond the borders of the Green Zone? And besides, the map reminded me that school was starting again next week.

I sat down on his bed (that was weird!) and looked around for something interesting to do. There was nothing so I lay back and closed my eyes. It was nice, lying there, hearing the scratch of his pencils as he wrote things on the page, smelling his odour. No, he wasn't smelly – I don't mean that kind of odour, just the smell or perfume or whatever it is that humans give off. It was warm and soothing like the turf my father brought home once and burnt. I felt totally relaxed and safe.

That's when your mind plays tricks, when your defences are down, because just then Mattie came marching right into my brain and the fact that he wasn't there with me became the biggest disappointment in the whole world and I rolled over and began to cry. Damian got up and put a blanket over me and then he lay down beside me and held me and said, 'Shh, shh, it's all right, everything will be fine, I promise.'

My little head was doing that triple processing thing that little heads do sometimes. In one part of my head I was sad thinking about Mattie; in another part of my head I was thinking, 'I'm lying on a bed with a boy who has his arms around me. This is interesting. This is nice. This is making me feel funny in funny places. I could get used to this.' And in the third part of my head I was thinking, 'How ridiculous that someone should promise you that everything will be fine. What kind of rubbish is that?'

Damian showed up in school on the first day back in the autumn. We still talk about four seasons here, even though there are really only two – four months of warmth and sun and then eight months of mild, wet weather. It doesn't get boring, though – the storms see to that. We have pretty fantastic storms. In the warm months they're electric. In the mild months, we get hurricane winds and wild, pelting rain. So although there are only two seasons, we still follow a four-season calendar and observe a school cycle that belongs to a time when children helped with sowing and harvesting crops, some time back in the Dark Ages. They teach us that stuff in history.

Anyway, on the first day of our new term, Damian was there. He wasn't tall, maybe a little taller than me, but he had an air of suppressed energy and strength that made people move out of the way when he walked towards them. His fifteenth birthday was coming up but not even the eighteen-year-olds bossed him around.

I suppose I was his only friend, though there was Pippa too, of course.

Oh, yes, Pippa. Pippa Petersen. Her family comes from some weird place in Scandinavia. They fled when the waters rose and flooded the fjord where they lived and swamped most of the northern countries, blah, blah, blah.

Anyway, she came speaking English with this ja-ja-ja accent and some kids in school gave her a hard time until I told one particularly irritating and totally random and irrelevant person to lay off. And because I'm the president's daughter the irrelevant person stopped annoying her. That's when Pippa attached herself to me and started following me around like some dim-witted servant creature who had formed an undying attachment to the first thing they saw in the world.

At first it was embarrassing. Come on, who needs a weird girl hanging out of them? Had I thrown a stick, she would have fetched it for me. Had I said, 'Take off all your clothes and jump in the school pond,' she would have done it. She was like my own personal dog, my blonde Scandinavian puppy. Even when I started being mean to her, calling her names, pinching her hard, she refused to go away. So then I just ignored her, but she became my shadow.

The funny thing was that Damian hit it off with her right from the start, from day one. He had this way of zoning in on people who were off most people's radar and talking to them like they were the most interesting person he'd met in ages and they were resuming a conversation they'd been having before. He had no time for the 'posh bastards', which basically was everyone else in the school, but he chatted away to Pippa and to the women who worked in the canteen serving our food.

And you know what? I was jealous – seriously jealous. I was the green-eyed monster. For two years I had never given Pippa a second thought in the beauty and allure department. She was just Pippa, quiet and shy in our incredibly dull school uniform. (Another rule to save civilisation.) And now here she was, pretty and perky and laughing with Damian, her blonde hair glistening and her eyes so, so blue and her skin translucent. (That's a word I really liked, from the moment I came across it in art appreciation: translucent.) When they were getting too lovey-dovey by half, I sent her on an errand to fetch a book from my locker. And you know what? Damian gave me one of his withering looks and said, 'Don't start acting like the queen bee of posh bastards. You're not like them.' I should have smacked him one. But I didn't. I blushed.

When Pippa came back I tried to study her, hoping she wouldn't notice, and I listened as Damian plied her with questions about her family and the journey they'd made here and who had been lost on the way. An uncomfortable question began to work its way into my brain and it was this: How come I'd never thought to ask Pippa any of this stuff? And what did my total lack of curiosity about Pippa's life say about me? Not a lot worth repeating. Pippa began to cry when she spoke of a grandfather and an aunt and uncle who hadn't survived the journey, and Damian put his arms around her and comforted her. And though students were not allowed to embrace or 'to engage in any form of intimate contact', no one stopped him. So there I was, sitting like a gooseberry as my two best 'friends' hugged each other. Brilliant.

At the end of the first day of the new term, I didn't even say goodbye to them; I just fled. In the car, I could see Geraldine was tense because she knew I was spoiling for a fight. And I was. I was just waiting for someone to give me an excuse, any excuse. But no one did.

The funny thing was that before I went to sleep, my mother came to my room and sat on my bed and didn't speak but stroked my face and kissed me on the forehead and said, 'Goodnight, my love,' in a voice I don't think I had ever heard her use before. When she closed the door I felt so sad and lonely that I cried myself to sleep.

Next day, everyone was tiptoeing around me – Francesca, Geraldine, Eddie the driver. I walked into school and when I saw Pippa, I said the first thing that came into my mind: 'Are you afraid you'll die and no one will love you?'

She didn't miss a beat but answered, looking me right in the eye, 'You love me.'

And know what? She couldn't have said anything nicer and for the second day in a row, someone broke the school rules by hugging Pippa Petersen.

Maybe now would be a good time to fill you in on our school. Its full name is Thomas Aquinas High School and it's a big rambling mansion with beautiful grounds around it, full of mature trees, so that arriving each day is like walking onto the set of a film. There is a primary school on the grounds in a smaller place they call the dower house.

The first time I heard that word I asked one of the teachers what it meant, and the answer she gave me went something like this: Well, suppose you're married to this rich gentleman and he dies and leaves all his wealth to your son; then the son gets married and the new wife takes one look at you and decides, that's it: the widow has to go. So your spineless son agrees and they build you a smaller house on the grounds to which you are banished. That's a dower house. It's like purgatory for unwanted widows. Kind of an ideal setting for a school, don't you think?

Of course, ours was an exclusive school for the Elite families, though some girls and a few totally irrelevant and random boys from the Green Zone are admitted when there are spaces, if their parents can afford to pay.

Each year three students are sponsored by the state to attend, from families in the Amber Zone. Pippa is an SSS (state-sponsored student). Being an SSS is an open invitation for other students to laugh at you, ridicule your social standing and sneer at your lack of wealth. The SSSes wear second-hand uniforms. Who could tell, you ask? Believe me, there's always someone who can tell. And the young teacher in charge of looking out for the SSSes has a little room behind the stage where she takes your measurements and fits you out.

So if you're unlucky enough to be a SSS in Thomas Aquinas, you might as well tie a placard around your neck and carry a stick for people to beat you with. Of course, everyone would deny that any of this is the case, but it's true. Which is why Pippa got such a rough time when she started here, and why she was so unbelievably grateful to me just for sticking up for her.

Pippa's family lived on the borders between the Green and the Amber Zones, up north, close to the great flood plains that separate the Green and Amber

Zones from the Badlands. So you can imagine the kerfuffle when I asked Mum if I could invite Pippa to stay for a weekend.

But they let her come, and for the second time in a few months, I holed up in a room with a friend and just went with the flow. I think my mother was really glad and relieved I had a friend: she came – not Francesca or Geraldine but my mother in person – with a tray of drinks and goodies. She did a good job of making Pippa feel welcome and making me feel I belonged to a nearly normal family.

Except she spoiled it by asking Pippa a zillion questions about her family. 'You have two older brothers, is that right? And your grandmother, how is she coping?'

And though she spoke in her soft little voice and was all smiling and sympathetic, I'd swear Mum had read everything that's in Pippa's file. There's a file on everyone, so you'd better watch yourself. Make sure you read the small print at the bottom of the advertisement for the job of 'friend to the president's daughter': The father reserves the right to send the Specials to check out your family and the mother reserves the right to read all about you in your private file. Hah!

However, to be fair to all concerned, Pippa seemed glad that my mum was interested in her and was as polite and well-mannered as I imagine it is possible for a person to be.

So what did we talk about in my room that weekend, away from the eyes and ears of watchful and listening adults? Damian, mostly, and Mattie, and fishing. It turned out my Pippa was really into fishing and knew all about lines and flies and casting and stuff that scouts know about. She learned survival skills up in the far north of Norway from a Sami hunter who was a friend of her father's.

'A who?' I said.

'A Sami.'

'Never heard of them.'

'Your education is sadly lacking for a president's daughter,' Pippa said.

That was something else about her that was new to me: this girl could answer back better than the smartest punks in school. It was weird. Two new friends – two real friends – in the space of a month and both start by giving me geography lessons.

The other thing we talked about was dogs. Pippa had a husky called Moonshine. She said he was like a brother to her and she adored him. Said it just like that, without any trace of self-consciousness or pretending to be cool. And I didn't say anything smart or clever, but just nodded, because I think I understood, even though I only have Eccles who is adorable in a cute kitty kind of way but I don't really adore her.

'Dogs see who you really are,' Pippa said. 'And once they attach to you, they stay loyal even if you are cruel or ignore them or want to send them away, because they know you are always more than the sum of your worst actions.'

She was focusing on stroking Eccles at the time and didn't see me blush because I knew she was really talking about me and her. And she knew I knew. But she didn't say it to make me feel small or humiliated, and though I felt like she'd slapped my wrist I also knew she forgave me and would forgive me for the small cruelties I'd inflicted on her.

The sad part of the Moonshine story is that Pippa had had to leave him behind when they left Norway. She dreams about him and in her sleep she hears him howling to the moon.

After lunch on Saturday we wandered in the grounds. Pippa said I lived in 'a seriously beautiful house' and she oohed and aahed at the formal garden and the fountains.

I suppose it is cool. And we do have pretty beautiful fountains. My favourite is the Triton. There he is, Mr Triton himself, in all his hairy, bearded splendour, surrounded by mermaids, sea-horses, dolphins and tortoises. And there's a fountain with a tangle of mermaids who represent the rivers of the State of Free Citizens: the Liffey, the Shannon, the Boyne, the Blackwater, the Blah-di-blah, all wrapped up together.

Beyond the formal gardens there is a parkland, and Pippa became something of a pain, naming every variety of tree that grows there and going on with all this hocus-pocus about the power of each tree and our sacred duty to preserve them. She gave me a mini-lecture on the importance of trees to the health of the planet and I felt like a bold girl about to be sent from the room for not paying attention or not taking the teacher seriously.

It was Pippa who suggested that we go to see the community that John 'founded' in the Valley of the Thrushes. John is my other brother. He's twelve years older than me. He'd been sent to school on a neighbouring island around the time I was born and when he came back, he had no real interest in me nor I in him. I had Mattie and didn't need anyone else.

Let's get this out of the way from the start: I didn't much believe in my brother John. I thought he was a big fake, with his 'heal the world' stuff and his alternative community and his long hair and his message of hope. I thought the people who called him a miracle-worker and who asked him to lay his healing hands upon their heads were mental. The way I saw it, he was in league with my father. There was something very fishy about the whole Pilgrim phenomenon.

All the same, I asked permission to visit with Pippa, and Mum asked Dad, and Dad told Mum that she could tell me that it was OK for me to visit and, yes, I could bring my friend.

That word, 'friend', sounded good coming from my father's mouth.

The Valley of the Thrushes is in the Green Zone, in the hills above the city. Geraldine came along, as usual, and we had a limousine to clear the road and we were waved through the checkpoints and up there before we knew it. Pippa said nothing but I could see she felt Very Important to be in a state car (actually it's my state car) and be waved through by the guards like we were some kind of royalty. The valley was beautiful, with two lakes and air that was really fresh and songbirds and herds of deer. I thought Pippa was going to die with happiness when she saw the deer.

John greeted us and brought us on a tour with the very pretty Gwen, both of them dressed in their ridiculous linen and wool tunics, like extras from those Biblical epics they used to make about a hundred years ago.

We kept pretty much to ourselves, not mixing with the ordinary members of the community. I don't know if Pippa noticed, but I did. It was a security thing, with my father's fingerprints all over it. You can be sure my dad's people spoke to John's people about the arrangements for our little visit: what was permissible and what was not. Geraldine would have been briefed too.

My attitude to the place was pretty sceptical, to put it mildly. To me it was just a trendy theme park for rich kids from Elite families, with John pretending to be some kind of Jesus or Saint Francis of Assisi.

Oh, sure, they had a chicken coop and the hens laid real eggs; there were sheep, and some of the girls were learning to spin yarn – an old woman was teaching them. They kept rabbits and pigeons like they did in medieval monasteries, and pigs and some cows for milking. They had created vegetable and fruit gardens and an orchard. And you could see all these vegetables that were native to this island, and then also the different kinds of vegetables we could grow because the climate had changed, blah, blah, blah.

But it didn't feel real. You knew that if all the crops failed and the animals died, no one would go hungry. You knew they'd never feel cold. If the whole place had been destroyed in a hurricane, they'd just have trooped down the hill to their families and gotten on with their lives.

Of course, the council supported this 'experimental community' and there was hardly a day went by without some great breakthrough or discovery being made by the Pilgrims and the research community that supported it. As if I believed any of that garbage. Pap for fools. Even the name was trite: 'the Pilgrims'. Hello? People, on the whole, are so utterly stupid and willing to believe everything they hear and see on the (very censored and controlled) daily news.

With the help of an army of engineers, researchers and scientists, the members of the commune had built these environment-friendly 'rondavels', which were neat circular thatched houses, with every luxury provided by solar and wind power. They had sweat lodges and saunas and hot pools and cold pools and any other kind of pool you like.

But what really, really wrecked my head was the mumbo-jumbo they all spewed out about saving the planet for future generations. Right. So sorry that half the planet is on fire, and that the ice caps have melted and the sea has flooded a third of the inhabitable land, but we hope that by dressing up in linen and home-spun wool and calling each other 'brother' and 'sister' we can really make a difference and turn things around. Yeah, right. So I wasn't the numero uno fan of the Pilgrim community. (I'm still not, but I was a bit OTT about it back then, truth be told.)

Pippa was really into everything, though, asking

what seemed like intelligent questions about yields and growing conditions and why they kept this animal and not that one and 'what would happen if' and 'what will happen when'. And anything John didn't know, a Pilgrim named Joshua answered. He seemed to me to be the brains behind the outfit. Gwen threw in puke-making comments like: 'Every seed we sow is a gift to Gaia.'

John and Gwen. Put me in mind of another four-letter word. If they were allowed to have babies, I thought they'd be the most ridiculously beautiful and stupid children that ever graced the planet. (Did I mention that you need permission from the council before you can bring a baby into the Citadel? No? Well, you do, because it's in the Book.)

After about an hour, John and Gwen were called away to greet a delegation from the Council of Free Citizens in New Zealand who were over visiting our government, and we were left with Joshua. He was very handsome. He told Pippa he came from Ethiopia and his family had been royalty before they lost much of their wealth. But not everything, obviously, because they had enough to pay for him to come to the Green Zone and live among the Elite. He spoke softly and his laughter was musical and his hands were fine and shapely. Pippa did all the talking, so I was free to observe and study them both, these foreigners walking the hills above the Citadel – black and white, south and north, male and female. It dawned on me that all her questions were for her family: what vegetables grow best in this climate? What do you add to the soil? Are the animals resistant to disease? Are the seeds genetically modified? Then she asked him a question that wiped the smile from his face: 'Will you use the knowledge you develop here to help the people in the Badlands?'

'All our work here will help preserve our civilisation and our people,' was the reply.

Wow! No fudge there.

Then Pippa asked the question I would have asked if I hadn't been the president's daughter and trained to keep my mouth shut: 'Who are "our people"?'

Joshua raised his head and looked at her. There was a hard edge to his voice. 'Everyone within our borders.'

'And those outside the borders of the Green Zone, all the people in the Amber Zone and the Badlands, what about them?'

He looked at her for a minute and I admired the way she met his gaze and held it as he tried to freak her out. 'It is not possible,' was what he said, after what seemed like a week.

'I don't see why not.'

You had to admire the girl's courage.

Joshua looked at Pippa with that funny expression that says, I know your type. You're a troublemaker and it has been noted.

You don't live the life I've led without recognising that look and realising that you'd better shut up pronto or you'll end up on a magical mystery tour that will end in the castle dungeon, the Hrad, at the bottom of the Citadel, and that's somewhere you don't want to be. Of course I've never been there, but I've never been dead or in hell either and I know they don't have much to recommend them.

So I grabbed Pippa by the arm and said, 'Boring, boring,' and 'Thank you, Joshua,' and dragged her away before someone else did.

Pippa was all indignant and stuttering and muttering until I pinched her really hard and said 'Shut up,' through clenched teeth and then she sort of got the message and reverted to her dog-like identity. I held on tight to her and brought her away from danger.

'Never ask a government official "why?" or "why not?" unless you are his superior. Do you want them to report you to the Specials? Do you want your family to have another visit from a Special? Use your head.'

Pippa broke free and pulled away and I noticed two things: (1) she was seething and (2) she had breasts.

The first didn't bother me but the second ... I was flat as a runway and she was all curvy and breasty, like a film star. I'd never noticed because in school she wears a uniform that looks like it came from the fat girls' shop. But here her top was tight and revealing, and I didn't like what it revealed.

'You have breasts,' I said, feeling instantly glum.

She looked at herself and shrugged. 'They just grew. Got nothing to do with me.'

Normally this sort of thing didn't bother me. I ignored the locker-room talk of 'racks' and 'pieces'. Being the president's daughter (with a personal guard keeping a discreet eye on things) protects you from the worst of bitchy comments and jock humour. But this was different. This was Pippa, my lapdog, my silent shadow, who, overnight, had developed (a) a personality, (b) good looks and allure and (c) breasts. It was depressing – which is partly why I told her she had been ridiculously stupid and naive to go pumping Joshua with questions and banging on about the poor people in the Badlands and she had, most probably, put her state sponsorship in doubt and her family in danger. OK, so the last bit was a tad over the top, but it felt good to let off steam and re-establish the status quo in our relationship, to show her (flat-chested though I might be) who was boss.

We sat down on a hill overlooking the camp and didn't say much for a long time. It should have been blissful, only Pippa was sniffling into her sleeve and clearly feeling sorry for herself. And to be honest, I was feeling guilty. I knew I'd been a shit.

'I don't think anything bad will happen, really,' I said, 'but you have to learn to be more careful. OK?'

She nodded.

'There's going to be a state reception for the New Zealand delegation. When we get back home, I mean. Would you like to come? We could pretend we're royalty.'

'They call you the princess, you know.'

'What? Who?'

'The people in the Badlands.'

'I'm not a princess.'

'To them you are.'

'What do they know about me?'

'More than you know about them.'

Ouch.

The weekend of the state reception for the New Zealand delegation, Pippa stayed over with me. Mum and Francesca made a fuss over finding just the right little dress for her to wear and suggesting how she should style her hair. They transformed her (using my clothes and my shoes) into a right princess.

Hello! Mother, Mother, hello! What about me? Your daughter? Hello, is anybody home? Way-hay, here I am …

But no – Pippa was their project, their new toy, their little orphan Annie, and they were having way too much fun to be bothered with boring old me.

I sulked, but what was the point? No one noticed. And then Pippa came over, all dressed for the ball, poor little Cinderella, and kissed me and told me I was her fairy godmother. We were reconciled – though actually she was too busy having a good time to realise we had fallen out.

And then at the reception in the castle (not the deep dark dungeons where the unspeakable things happened), there was a repeat performance of oohs and aahs, and we were surrounded by all the cooing ladies in their designer dresses, glittering with jewels.

I usually enjoy these kinds of occasions, if only for the secret pleasure I take in laughing at what passes for style among the 300. Come on, who ever said having money is the same thing as having taste or flair? Normally I'm cracking up at these dos, splitting my sides at the parade of fashion disasters. I pick out the ridiculously skinny wives who totter around on stiletto heels while their fat husbands stuff their mouths with food. And then I give time to scrutinising the one or two seriously stylish women who pass among us (and one or two seriously handsome men, but then they are way too old for me).

Also, I like attracting the admiring gaze of those unfortunates who recognise my sense of style. I do know how to dress. That's not vanity; I'm just stating a fact. It's also a fact that ninety-nine per cent of people don't know how to dress.

Not that my impeccable dress sense mattered a whit that evening, because all the busy bees were buzzing around Pippa, and Mum was acting like she had rescued her from the animal shelter and trained her to be human. When some of the New Zealanders arrived and asked Mum if 'this beautiful young lady' was her daughter, I'd had enough. I made a mental note: never, ever become the president's wife. Unless, that is, you want to devote yourself to idiotic projects and spend days and months of your life saying inane things to inane people.

Then my father appeared and took my arm and excused us, saying he wanted me to meet some people. He smiled at Mum and she smiled at him and then he steered me towards a group of men who were standing in a circle, with Specials hovering close by. This was the centre of power.

'Gentlemen, I'd like you to meet my daughter, Valentina.'

My God, what was happening? My father acting like my knight in shining armour, saving me from the clutches of the living dead.

I shook hands and nodded to those I recognised and said polite welcomes to the visiting dignitaries.

'Did you enjoy your visit to the Valley of Thrushes?' I asked one visitor whom I recognised from our trip to see Holy John.

I suppose at this point I should write something on the weirdness of my father, as a father and as a human being. He is weird, make no mistake. He's been president of the State of Free Citizens from the time I was a little girl. In fact, I can't remember the time before he became president, when he was just my dad. Being president makes him weird – he's never off duty; even at home with me and my mother, I never really know what he's thinking. But that night, the night at the reception for the New Zealanders, I enjoyed being with him and I saw how everyone in that circle listened to every word he said. And I saw how little he said, so they were never quite sure what he thought of any of them. They were anxious to win his praise and they all treated me as if I was the most interesting girl they had ever met. I made another mental note (I take a lot of mental notes): learn the art of inscrutability from your father. It makes you mysterious, which is useful.

After we entered the Great Hall for dinner, we sang our hymn. We're big on Christianity here. Well, not me personally, but the State of Free Citizens owes its deliverance from the terrible floods to our Christian God. Haven't you read the Book? The public religion is Christianity, praise the Lord. What you do in private is your own business but if you come as a guest to our state, you sing the hymns like everybody else.

Pippa did not sit with our family. She was seated with some random guests. I was glad. She was my friend, but she wasn't family and that night I didn't want her to be family. (Does that make me as mean as it sounds?)

I looked over to her between courses, and each time she was deep in conversation with this very important looking prince or king. He was dressed in a splendid blue and gold embroidered gown, with a headdress made of feathers. And he wore a sparkling earring that caught the light. He was like a fantastic peacock.

Once, when I looked over to them, our eyes met and he smiled and bowed in my direction and I nearly fell off my chair. The exotic peacock prince was Joshua! Joshua of the Pilgrims. Joshua of the Valley of the Thrushes. Joshua who gave Pippa one of those eyebrow-raising looks when she'd asked more questions than was wise. Joshua who was a Special if ever I saw one!

My brain went into overdrive. What was going on? Think, brain, you fat idle loaf! What was going on? I looked at my father. Why had he put Pippa sitting there? Was Joshua doing a little bit of espionage for my father? I hoped Pippa Peterson wasn't being her annoying self, asking too many questions or making silly suggestions that might be regarded as 'a danger to the smooth functioning of our orderly society'.

Sure, it was a right pain to have little Goldilocks Pippa prancing around in my clothes with my mother slobbering all over her, but she was still my friend, my best friend, and I didn't want her carted off to the darkest dungeon in the castle because she didn't know when to keep her big mouth shut. See, being infuriatingly intelligent and a know-all isn't all it's cracked up to be when you lack some basic cop-on, like knowing when to button it. Speaking your intelligent thoughts in the wrong place could land you in a dungeon surrounded by Specials intent on 'protecting our way of life from dangerous and invidious elements intent on causing anarchy and fuelling social unrest'. (You don't get to be the president's daughter without picking up some of the lingo.)

Right now, I hoped she was saying the kinds of silly things to Joshua that most of the women in the room might have said: Oh, you look so lovely. Blue is such a royal colour. Your feather hat is just divine. Oh my God, I'd die for an earring like that. You really must introduce me to your designer.

Please, Pippa, don't mention waterborne diseases in the Badlands or the potential of new varieties of seed to feed everyone on the island or any of the other things that fill your lovely, twisted mind. Please.

6

The next week, the week after the ball, was strange. Or maybe I was strange. I felt strange. I felt as if things were happening, things were changing, things that would affect me, and I was waiting for the sign that said: 'If you are waiting for a sign, this is it. Do what you must do and do it now.'

I think the main reason was, I was unsettled by the whole thing of my dad including me in the business end of things at the reception. Something had been set in motion. Yeah, I know this sounds like rubbish – light the incense and wait for the spirit guides – but this was how I felt. Stuff was happening and I was part of it and it felt as if I was meant to be part of it. You know that feeling? This is fate or destiny.

And I felt I was growing up, too. All of a sudden, I wanted to know more about things, things I hadn't bothered about before, things that hadn't seemed important but now seemed the most important things in the world. Pippa, for example. I wanted to know exactly where she came from and how she got here. That was the sort of stuff I would have talked over with Mattie and he wouldn't have thought me weird and he would have helped me make sense of it. But there was no Mattie – and I wanted to know what he was doing. Why he had left. What he thought about things.

I don't know why all these things suddenly seemed so urgent – maybe it was a growth spurt in my brain or something – but I wanted to eat up the world and all it contained. I was hungry for knowledge, and on edge. But you can't eat knowledge so I did the next best thing – I ate chocolates and chocolate fudge cake and peanuts. I ate till I was sick and threw up and then I hated myself but the hunger came back so I stuffed myself with everything I could find. But it didn't satisfy me.

I'm not an eating-disorder kind of girl, so this was weird. I can't explain it. It was as if I sensed that something was about to happen, but I can't say how I knew or why it upset me so badly.

People seemed to twig that I was going through a bad patch. They gave me a wide berth. I stayed in my room and the world left me alone. In school, I hardly saw Pippa or Damian. I went to class, ate my lunch without saying too much and left immediately afterwards. They didn't make a big deal of it. They didn't ask me annoying questions or try to cheer me up or pretend to be all happy-clappy. They just let me be.

Geraldine was all attentive. But not in an irritating 'Oh, shit, my job's on the line' kind of way. I think she was really looking out for me and that was sweet.

One night, about a week after the ball, I went down to my mother's room. I was loitering outside, debating with myself, when she called out.

'Is that you, Francesca?'

'No, it's me.'

'Valentina?'

I could hear the surprise in her voice. Half of me wanted to say something smart and run away, but I managed to keep my mouth shut. My mum appeared and smiled.

'Come in.'

I sat down in one of the matching armchairs she had near her desk. There was a fire in the grate and everything seemed cosy. She put away what ever she had been studying and sat opposite me.

'Let's have some tea,' she said and rang for Francesca. 'You made quite an impression at the reception, Val,' she said. 'Your father was so proud of you.'

'Thank you.'

Then she said something that surprised me.

'You're so like Mattie.'

'But you don't like Mattie.'

'Good gracious, Valentina, what a ridiculous idea! Who ever put such a notion in your head?'

'But you didn't try to stop him leaving.'

'Oh, Valentina, Valentina.' She shook her head and looked into the fire and she had such a sad expression that I knew immediately I had it wrong.

'Sorry,' I said, and Mother smiled at me but I could tell her thoughts were far away.

Francesca came with the tea and we sat and chatted about the reception and the New Zealand delegation and other safe little subjects. And all the questions I had intended to ask my mother remained unspoken, and all the vague unformed feelings remained unformed.

When it was time for me to go to bed, Mum kissed me on the forehead.

'I enjoyed our little chat, Val. Thank you.'

I went to my room and I was tired, but it was hours before I fell asleep.

It must have been the chat with my mother: the next day in school, I felt calm and serene.

After English class (my favourite subject) I went to the canteen for lunch. Damian came rushing in, wild-eyed, shouting for me and acting in a way that was really scary. Pippa sat next to me and though she was better than anyone I know at not showing what she thought, I saw that she too was alarmed as Damian ran the length of the canteen looking for us. He threw himself into a chair opposite us and looked from one of us to the other, as if he expected a reaction. I'm not sure about Pippa, but I didn't know what I was supposed to do or say.

'Haven't you heard?' he said, with a show of impatience.

'Heard what?'

'Greenland. The ice cap.'

'What are you talking about, Damian?'

He sat back and his whole body trembled with anger or frustration or some other negative emotion.

'What?' I said, speaking low, because the president's daughter doesn't raise her voice in public. 'Don't sit there and give me that look. I don't know what you are on about.'

'Greenland,' he repeated. But at least he was talking quietly and making an effort to stay calm.

'What about it?'

'Most of the ice has crashed into the sea. There's been a massive quake.'

'So?'

'So? Is that all you can say?'

'What? What am I supposed to say?'

'Haven't you been listening to me? Didn't you hear what I just said?'

Now he was talking way too loud and there were six hundred ears trying to eavesdrop on us. I ignored them.

'Yes, I heard what you said,' I answered, deliberately speaking very quietly in an effort to thwart the curious masses. 'A quake in Greenland. Greenland. Two thousand miles away.' (Two thousand was the first number that came into my head but it must have been pretty accurate because neither Damian nor the walking encyclopaedia that was Pippa contradicted me.) 'Actually, I think we're quite safe. So, if you don't mind, I would like to finish my lunch, thank you. And I don't think there is any need for you to shout at me.' I shook my head and turned away from him to say something to Pippa but she looked like someone who had just received bad news – really bad news. She was stricken.

'It's not such a big deal, Pippa,' I said, furious at Damian for causing a commotion.

'It is, Val,' she answered, whispering in a little voice that was not like her own voice at all.

'Why?' I asked, beginning to feel seriously annoyed.

'Because if it's true, it will be like Noah's flood. Hundreds of towns and cities will be flooded. Maybe even here.'

'Here? In the Citadel?'

'No. But in the west and on the floodplains …'

She didn't have to finish her sentence. I knew she was thinking about her family.

'Look, there's been nothing, absolutely nothing, on the news. If this was as big a deal as you are saying, it would have to be on the news. Right?'

Damian looked at me with a scornful expression.

'You of all people, Valentina, should know how things work here.'

'Excuse me? Firstly, when did you start calling me "Valentina"? And secondly, what's that supposed to mean?'

'It means your father and his friends won't let

the citizens hear or see what's going on in the real world, because you live in the wonderful Green Zone, where all your dreams come true. You know what I'm talking about.'

'If there's control of the news, then it's for a good reason.' Yeah, I know, I was starting to sound like my father. I just didn't want to face all this stuff.

'A good reason for lying? Let me think about that.' His tone was poisonous and his look was worse. 'What about power and control? Are they good enough reasons?'

'A good reason is not wanting the citizens to worry over things they cannot control,' I said, like a good president's daughter.

'That's just bullshit,' he said, like a real feral boy.

I was aware of the general intake of breath in the dining hall among the students who were desperately pretending that they were not listening to every word being spoken at our table. Shouting 'bullshit' into the face of the daughter of the president in front of the whole school was not a good career move, at least not at that time in our country's history. Let's say that a great silence fell upon the canteen and Geraldine, trusty and true and totally tuned in (pretty good alliteration, even if I say so myself) moved in pretty smartly and a school monitor tapped Damian on the shoulder.

'280C, you are required in the principal's office now.'

Damian threw him a filthy look. 'I'm coming.' And then he leaned in close and hissed at Pippa, 'You tell her. Make her understand.'

***

That night, Mum came to see me.

'Is everything all right, Valentina?'

Now, me and my dear old mum had had something of a breakthrough in diplomatic relations – well, it was more than diplomatic relations – and I didn't want to spoil things but, let's be honest, old habits die hard. I hate when people ask questions to which they already know the answer – as if Geraldine hadn't made a full report. So I reverted to my 'fine' approach.

'Fine,' I said, with great emphasis and conviction. And just in case she hadn't got the message, I repeated it. 'Fine.'

'There was a commotion in school?'

'Your feral boy used a bad word and people got excited.'

'Whatever else he is, Valentina, he is certainly not my feral boy.'

'Oh! So whose idea was it to take him on as a little project and make him safe for civilised society?'

'I have no idea what you are talking about, Valentina.'

Now, my mother was the original ice lady and it wasn't often that you heard things like irritation in her voice. But I heard it then so I needled her a little more.

'Oh, yes, you do,' I said. 'His parents wanted your help in re-educating him. Remember?'

'As I recall, they sought your assistance and you gave it of your own volition.'

'No. As I recall, it was your idea.'

Mother sighed, not a great big histrionic sigh, more of a little controlling sigh, one that said, Don't let this silly child get under your skin. You are the adult and she is just an annoying teenager. Then, having regained her president's wife's demeanour, she continued. 'But I'm so glad the incident in school has not upset you, my dear.'

Yuck. Is there a more annoying, irritating term of endearment than 'my dear'? I don't think so. And then, to make matters worse, she moved as if to kiss my cheek but I was too quick for her and I dropped my head so that she planted her kiss in my hair.

Night, night, sweet Mama. Go now. Leave. Disappear. Leave me alone.

And as if by magic, she did.

In school the next day there was no sign of Damian. The headmistress, Ms Iris Rumsfeld, sent word for me to visit her office. Poor Ms Rumsfeld. How she grovelled. The school was most fortunate to have the president's daughter, blah, blah, blah. How distressed she was to think that another student … blah, blah, blah. On and on she droned.

Now, power and control – the subjects upon which Damian and I had our little contretemps – are interesting phenomena. And when you realise that you wield them over someone, a certain pleasure arises. I don't state this as a matter of pride, just as a matter of fact.

I enjoyed myself in her office. I did not react to anything she said. I was Valentina the Inscrutable, daughter of the Great Inscrutable. Every time she paused, waiting for me to acknowledge the most laudable sentiments she was expressing, I stared at the wall; blank, indifferent and cruel. I know it's not nice to say this and it does not reflect well on me, but here goes: the old windbag made me laugh inside. And then she said something about ensuring that Damian would never return to the school and I reacted.

'No,' I said, very quietly and very firmly. 'Why would you expel a friend of mine who wanted to inform me of matters of national importance?'

Poor old Rumsfeld crumbled to pieces and began blathering on and on. I didn't wait for any more, but rose from my seat, thanked her and left, closing the door behind me.

All down the corridor I felt the thrill of exercising power, pulling rank, of behaving like an insufferable prig!

I was on a roll. I saw Pippa and commanded her to come to my house for the weekend. I told her she had to brief me on the Greenland situation. The next day, when Damian, subdued and watchful, reappeared, I told him he was to come too. Oh, yes, Valentina, the spoilt princess who must be obeyed. OK, I'm not proud of this, but at the time it felt very good.

I expected some reaction, some edict from on high forbidding the devil child from visiting, such as 'Now, Valentina, there are some things that we simply cannot tolerate. You know this. We do have our standards and the 300 families must set an example, live by the Book.'

Each time I met my mother, I braced myself for the attack. But there was nothing: no mention of the episode in school, no mention of my visit to Ms Rumsfeld. And when Pippa and Damian arrived, Mother called after a while and made polite conversation. Could it be that she hadn't heard, that Geraldine had kept quiet, and Ms Rumsfeld, too? Could it be that the tentacles of the octopus could only reach so far?

It was a comforting thought, but one I did not really entertain. After all, I was dealing with my parents and nothing escaped them. Nothing. But it was a delicious thought that I might slip through their net and roam about the world unattended. Delicious but totally without foundation.

Damian was subdued and Pippa had reverted to her lapdog identity. There we were in my room (the sitting-room part which looks out on the garden) and I pulled the strings and they danced to my every move. I have a chaise longue in my room – purple with great ruby velvet cushion; very chic even if I say so myself – and I arranged myself on the chaise while Pippa explained all about the ice and the earthquake and the likely effects.

As she spoke in her earnest little voice, I sat like a queen who has the power to bestow favour or take a life. I asked one or two pertinent questions (just to remind them of my penetrating intelligence) and listened attentively. Pippa spoke slowly and carefully, weighing every word, and I could see she was frightened of the story she told.

Damian threw in comments or took over at times but, whereas Pippa was slow and clear, he was all rushed and confused, as if his thoughts raced too quickly for his mouth, and I said encouraging things like, 'Well, that was very helpful, thank you; I'm sure someone, somewhere, might figure out what it is you are trying to say.'

And then the eyes of my devil-child flared with anger but he had learned that there are consequences for shouting at me, so he fell into a sullen silence and Pippa picked up where she had left off.

When all was said and done, the picture was pretty clear: a lot of people – thousands of people, maybe even hundreds of thousands – were going to lose their lives and their livelihoods.

When Feral Boy and Northern Girl had finished telling me the news of the world as they claimed it to be, I told them it was time for lunch. I had arranged it all, choosing the menu myself: chicken soup, followed by a selection of cold meats, salads and freshly baked bread. Dessert was a chocolate mousse, which was one of Bridget's specialities. (Bridget is our cook, one of the original Tribe.)

The table was all set up in the conservatory which overlooks the Triton fountain. It looked brilliant – modern and sophisticated.

Pippa has a natural sense of style and can wear any old thing and look terrific. Damian, on the other hand, hasn't a clue and never will have – not about clothes, not about table manners, not about the small things that make life … well, civilised. (Yes, I know I'm sounding like my mother but she has a point.)

Francesca brought our food. She was all smiles to Pippa and they spoke about the night of the reception and Pippa thanked her and Francesca said she was lovely and Pippa thanked her again and Francesca said she was lovely again – it made me want to throw up.

And no sooner was the soup served than Damian was hunched over it, slurping up the contents of his bowl, totally oblivious to the sounds he was making and his disgusting way of chewing and swallowing. So all in all it was more like the Mad Hatter's tea party than the kind of occasion I had planned. When he raised his head and saw me looking at him, he got all defensive.

'What?' he said.

'You are not a pig, Damian. You could at least pretend that you are civilised.'

'The world is collapsing, people are dying, the planet might never recover and all you can think about are table manners?'

I did my best Mother imitation. 'I don't think the collapse is quite as imminent as you predict. And what's happening a few thousand miles away in the ocean does not excuse your disgusting behaviour here. Or maybe in that warped little head of yours, you really believe that eating like a savage will save the planet? Grow up.'

My God, I really was being a perfect bitch. But he was so annoying.

He looked to Pippa for support, but she was keeping her head down and refusing to play the game. (Well, it was a game. A kind of courtship ritual that I was trying out for the first time.)

'You're so right,' he snarled. 'Sitting around here playing the little princess is just what the world needs right now. Why didn't I think of it sooner?'

'If you don't like the company, the food or the way we do things here, you can leave. And then we can eat our lunch in peace.'

'Peace. Whose peace? Your peace, with your dainty little table manners.'

Now here I have to make a confession. I got what Damian was on about. I mean, I understood where he was coming from. But he was so sure of himself, so arrogant and dismissive of others that I wasn't going to give him the satisfaction of agreeing with him. No way.

So I gave him the queen bee treatment: that's when you don't look at the person you're talking to because you're so above them it would offend your eyes to have to see them. Speak with great remoteness. Be exasperated. Say everything as if you were explaining it to a very young child.

'Table manners may not seem very important to you, but they are essential in any civilised community. Table manners tame the animal in us. They are the product of reason. Your way of eating is the product of an uncontrolled appetite. If you ruled the world, we'd all tear lumps out of each other fighting over our food. The whole world would be like the Badlands.'

Even if I say so myself, I thought that was a pretty good little speech. But then I heard myself in my head and I sounded like my mother, which was alarming, because I wasn't trying to sound like her that time. Oh my God. What greater horror than sounding like your mother when you think you're being yourself! And for the second time in twenty-four hours. It was turning into a disaster. I really wasn't not very good at courtship rituals.

'Well, you might find it amusing to sit here and make fun of me, but I have better things to be doing with my time.'

'Like what?'

'Like going to the other zones to help people.'

At this point, Pippa's head popped up like a regular cuckoo in a clock. 'The Amber Zone?'

'And beyond, if needs be.'

'You'd go to the Badlands?' Pippa asked, and I could hear the tremor in her voice and the excitement too.

'Yes. Want to come?'

'Will you take me?'

'It won't be a picnic.'

At this point, my patience was exhausted.

'Listen to the two of you. "Yes, let's go to the Badlands. We'll take the bus. What a jolly adventure it will be." Get real. There's no way you'll get to the Badlands. Anyway, you don't know if anything unusual is happening. You've heard reports from

55

your mysterious sources. If – and it's a big if – if the Greenland icecap has jumped into the sea and created an earthquake and the whole world now stands – drumroll – on the edge of disaster, how come there hasn't been a dicky bird in any of the news reports? Or maybe you're just in love with the idea of disaster and rushing off to save the planet? Meet Damian, Planet Boy.'

I began to laugh till the tears rolled down my face. I was enjoying myself. Do you know how sometimes when you get on a roll and you're really amusing yourself, you forget that others might not find you as outrageously funny as you find yourself? Well, that was one of those moments.

I was just about to launch into a speech on Planet Boy when I saw Damian's face. It was crimson.

OK, Valentina, I said to myself, time to back off before Damian EXPLODES.

It was Pippa, using her little servant-girl voice, who spoke.

'The Greenland story is true.'

'Who verified the reports?'

'Joshua confirmed it for me.'

'Joshua of the Pilgrims? Of the ball?'

'Yes.'

'You spoke to Joshua?'

'Yes.'

'You know he's an agent, a Special?'

'He was very nice to me at the reception.'

I said nothing to this. This information needed to be processed. Joshua! My God, he was old enough to be her father. Well, maybe not quite, but near enough.

'Ask your father, if you don't believe it,' Damian said, less crimson now but still in a huff.

'If it has not been reported in the news, my father will hardly confirm it, will he?'

'Ah, so you do know how things work here in the State of Free Citizens.'

I said nothing. I sat looking out on the garden. It was as calm and manicured as ever.

'It's hard to believe that some disaster has happened and half the island is affected,' I said.

'Come with me then; I'll show you,' Damian said, full of manly courage.

'You are being ridiculous.'

'You just don't want to face the fact that not everyone lives like you. You're too attached to this way of life.'

To be fair to the boy, it was a good line but it didn't make me feel guilty or upset. It just made me angry.

'I must be missing something here. Aren't you Damian from family 280? So you're hardly living in the slums, are you? And if my memory serves me right, it was your family who paid to come to live in the Citadel, to escape from the chaos beyond our borders, so don't lecture me on the way we live here as if it has nothing to do with you and your family.'

'I've been there. I know what I've seen.'

'Well, good for you. And now you're back and happy to be, for all your talk. You're just as much a part of this as I am or Pippa is, for that matter. So screw you.'

Pippa blushed. I had them on the run.

After a long time, Damian spoke.

'Yeah, I might be part of all this, but I want to join Solidarity and see if I can help them in their work with refugees. And if you wanted to do more than live like a spoilt little rich girl, you would too. Or maybe you're ashamed of your brother and what he does?'

He meant Mattie. He's with Solidarity.

'You've no right to speak about my brother; no right at all. In fact, I want you to leave now; just go. You're a prick.'

'That's right. Play the hurt little princess.'

Before he said another word, I slapped him hard across the face. And I didn't feel sorry for one moment. He'd gone too far.

'How dare you!' I said.

No one spoke for what seemed like an age.

'At least go and see Joshua and find out what's really happening,' Damian said at last.

I didn't answer, and he didn't leave.

And then, with impeccable timing, Mum appeared. She flashed a smile all around and then, sensing the tension in the air, narrowed her eyes. 'You're very quiet,' she said, scrutinising us all.

I couldn't think of anything smart to say, but then Pippa piped up.

'We've just been discussing the idea of spending some time in the Pilgrim community. Do you think that's a good idea, Mrs O'Connor?'

My mother gave her fixed-smile look. 'I think that's a splendid idea. You'd all learn so much. I'll mention it to Valentina's father.'

I smiled back my fixed smile and my mother fluttered away.

I was furious with Pippa. She'd set me up. She'd no right to say that to my mother. I was so angry I was afraid to speak, so I was taking deep breaths and counting to ten in my head. When I felt I could trust myself, I spoke.

'If it can be arranged, we'll spend a weekend with my brother and the Pilgrims. And I will speak with Joshua. In the meantime, please do not speak to me of Greenland or rumoured global disasters or any other eco-fairytales.'

And then, because I was thoroughly sick of the sight of them, I sent them packing.

I spent the rest of the evening and most of the following day going through my wardrobe. Later in the week, over dinner, Mum raised the question of me, Pippa and Damian spending a weekend with the Pilgrims. Dad repeated the two names and said 'Hmm.' Then he gave me a brief, sharp look. This response could have meant any number of things, including:

(a) Damian was dead meat

(b) Damian and his family would receive a visit from the Specials

(c) Pippa was dead meat

(d) Pippa and her family would receive another visit from the Specials

(e) I'll think this over

(f) That's fine.

I knew better than to ask for clarification.

Almost a week passed and nothing was said. And then Mother mentioned, in a casual, offhand way, that everything had been arranged for my 'little trip' the following weekend.

I can't explain why, but the news sent me into a panic. I began pulling out clothes that I'd need for the weekend, and then pulling out more and more – ridiculous, unsuitable clothes, the best clothes in my collection, touching them, feeling the fabric as if I might never see them again.

Francesca found me in floods of tears, lying on my bed, my clothes pulled around me in a protective mound.

'I don't know what to bring,' I sobbed, and no amount of gentle words could console me.

In the end, Mother and Francesca chose my clothes and Father looked in too, saying, 'I want you to be as inconspicuous as possible, Valentina – no make-up, no expensive clothes or jewellery, nothing that will draw attention to yourself.'

'Why?'

'Because it is not a time to flaunt your wealth or your privilege.'

Sometimes my father's replies were like rifle shots: loud, sharp and dangerous. 'You will have security but it will be discreet. You'll travel to the camp in the way that any other group of students would travel there. This time you will mix freely with the other community members and John will treat you as he would treat anyone visiting the community. Do nothing and say nothing to draw attention to yourself. Understand?'

I nodded.

'Will I give the same message to Pippa and Damian?'

'That will not be necessary.'

I nodded. I wondered who had been sent to brief them.

It should have been an exciting adventure but my father's instructions made me uneasy. Why was he taking such a hands-on approach, giving me explicit instructions?

The Valley of the Thrushes was a communications-free zone and I didn't look forward to a whole weekend without my beautiful, mobile technological friend. If I had the means I would have turned back the clock twelve months when life had seemed much less complicated and serious.

The night before our visit, I tossed and turned and had the strangest dreams. In one I was lost in a desert landscape. After endless searching I saw a house and ran to it for shelter, but it was empty and the roof was missing. In another, I was in a small boat navigating a wild river. At any moment it seemed the boat would capsize, but I was terrified of the water – it was full of unspeakable things and the smell was putrid. The stench was still in my nose when I woke up.

I felt strange, almost like a different person, in the clothes I was wearing for my trip to the Valley of the Thrushes. Mum had found an old sweater of Mattie's. At first I didn't want to wear it but later I was glad I had. It gave me courage. I also wore an old pair of tracksuit bottoms and runners. For the first time in God knows how long, I had no make-up on – I mean no make-up. All you could see was this pasty-faced little girl with a pony-tail in oversized, shapeless clothes. It was like going around undressed.

My change of clothes, a warm jacket, my diary and some protein bars were in a small backpack. This was new, but Francesca trod on it in the flowerbed to make it seem less so.

The arrangements (they had been made on my behalf) were for me to meet Pippa and Damian at the West Shopping Centre. Eddie drove me with Geraldine. It was weird, not least because Mum had hugged me and kissed me before I left and Geraldine seemed on edge. Did they know something that I didn't?

From the shopping centre we took the tram towards the south-west rim of the Citadel. I'd never been on a tram before – Pippa and Damian showed me how to buy a ticket. I even carried my backpack into the carriage all by myself. Well, that's a big deal if you're not used to doing these things. Come on, credit where credit is due.

I had been nervous about leaving my comfort zone but I have to admit that on the tram I felt OK and almost normal for one of the first times in my life. I sat and watched the world passing and stared at the people on the platforms waiting for trams. Most seemed happy; if there were thousands of people killed by a terrible quake, it wasn't affecting the mood of the people I saw.

Some caught my eye and smiled. One girl, a little younger than me, smiled so sweetly I wanted to run out and hug her. And then I became aware that Damian was watching me and, though I tried to ignore it, it's pretty hard to pretend someone isn't watching you when you know they are. He was sitting opposite me, and Pippa was on the seat beside me. It was unusual for me to sit so close to someone who wasn't Mattie, and it made me feel better. Pretty soon I realised I was holding her hand and I didn't want to let go and I didn't want to be the queen bee either.

'We're nearly there,' Damian said. His voice was so soft and kind, I forgot I was angry with him for forcing me into this trip and gave him a big smile. And then he did something that stunned me – he leaned over and kissed me on the cheek. Ordinarily, I might have slapped his face or given him a piece of my very-bitchy-when-it-needs-to-be mind, but I just sat in my seat, leaned back my head, closed my eyes and tried to hold the moment. Jesus, I thought to myself, I think I'm falling in love.

And then all those trips to the National Art Gallery with my father when I was young came back to haunt me, because Caravaggio's *The Taking of Christ* came into my mind. You know the one – Judas kisses Jesus on the cheek and it's a sign for the soldiers to move in and seize him. I didn't want to be thinking like that – I wanted the Happy Thoughts to kick the hell out of the Bad Thoughts, and I told myself that they had but they hadn't really and my moment of feeling in love was shadowed by the idea of betrayal. So here's the question: Is this normal stuff to have in your head or am I a big freak?

John, Gwen and Joshua were there to meet us and this must have been a little bit unusual because the other three passengers, who were regular visitors to the community, were really excited and treated John as if he was some rock star and came over all silly and oh-my-God-ish when he embraced them and welcomed them as brother and sister. Even Pippa and Damian were a little in awe and starstruck. When it was his turn to welcome me his hug was warmer and more genuine than I expected and he called me 'sister' in a way which made me realise that my coming to stay meant something to him.

Gwen was really sweet – not in an annoying way, just really nice. I had been expecting the worst and had been filled with dread about this trip but it was turning out to be just the opposite to what I had imagined, so I did the most un-me thing imaginable: I burst into tears.

It was so embarrassing. However, it had one unintended outcome – one of the older girls put her arm around me and told me not to worry, that meeting John for the first time often had this effect on young Pilgrims. So at least my disguise was working. And even though I was blubbering like a baby, I still had enough of my wits about me to realise that Pippa was all weak-kneed and cute-little-girly whenever Joshua opened his mouth and I thought that was pretty disgusting. Hey, I mean, it's all right for me, a fourteen-year-old, to get a little hot and bothered by a fifteen-year-old, but Joshua was positively old, maybe even double her age, and that was just downright wrong, bordering on the perverted. I used to think Pippa the most sensible girl on the planet. There is no accounting for the effects of hormones on the impressionable young mind and, even more alarming, on the impressionable young body.

After the greetings and the welcome we were shown to our quarters – this amazing rondavel which was so cool. (Yeah, I know I was supposed to hate everything about this false community but hey, the place was fantastic. Somewhere can be fantastic and false, right?) Each person had his or her own private little space for their possessions, and a small loo, because even Pilgrims have to pee and stuff. The washroom was shared but there was a strong door that you could lock, which was good. No, I'm not paranoid, but the bathroom is private, right? It's not my idea of fun waking up to the sight of other people's dangly bits in the morning when all you want to do is take a shower in peace. In the largest rondavel, they have communal wash facilities but no way would I even consider that, no way in the whole wide world.

Anyway, in our rondavel, built for six, there was a stove in the centre and around this was what the Pilgrims called the Circle of Brotherhood (sisterhood was a bit down the pecking order in the community, but I'll get to that later), where you ate and talked and then slept on a little mat, in your sleeping bag. When I raised the obvious question about boys and girls sleeping side by side, John explained that this was a Circle of Trust and anyone who violated the trust was expelled from the community.

'So,' I said, 'this is like a religious community and no one has sex?'

John smiled and he almost looked intelligent. 'Couples who pledge themselves before the community have their own quarters.'

'So the other rondavels are like the singles club?'

'They're communal. You'll get the hang of it quickly enough.'

'So who'll be sharing our rondavel?'

'Just you and your friends, if you are happy with that.'

'Yeah, I guess,' I answered, though I wasn't really sure I was happy. Pippa, yes – no problem there – but Damian? Did I really want him that close to me or me that close to him?

When John was satisfied that I was settled in, he left us in the care of Joshua and another Pilgrim who had the same kind of relationship to him that Pippa had with me when we first met – a lapdog. The lapdog's name was Thomas and though he said all the right things, smiled and seemed ever so helpful and spoke ever so politely, he gave me the creeps. You know how you can meet someone and you know from the first moment that you'll love them for ever? Though, to be perfectly honest, that's never happened to me, but you know what I'm saying: some people give off a good vibe. Others smell. Well, Thomas was one of those people who smells. And just having him around me made me feel all itchy and uncomfortable and in need of a shower and a change of clothes. If the others felt the same, they didn't say it or show it so I tried to ignore him as best I could, which, in fairness, wasn't that hard because he seemed to me to be another of those totally irrelevant and random human beings that populate the planet.

Joshua gave us the Pilgrim scarf to wear: it's a double-loop scarf that you can wear as a headdress – very ethnic and global and PC – and it was warm, actually. Everyone had to wear it at all times in the community.

Now, one thing I had learned in my short life is that there are always rules and codes and limitations. Just because everyone called each other brother and sister, and love was the drug of choice, and everything was very hippy and eco and chilled, it didn't mean there were no guards and no surveillance. There were guards everywhere. After a while you just knew who they were.

The weekend and visiting Pilgrims wore their regular clothes but the resident Pilgrims dressed in long woven shirts and what looked like pyjama bottoms, so that they might have been a bunch of refugees from India. Over their shirts they wore woollen or leather tunics. It wasn't exactly a riot of colour up there in the Valley of the Thrushes.

All those loose-fitting garments should have made it easy for the guards to conceal their weapons but, being the president's daughter, I spotted them a mile off. I'm not boasting, I'm just stating the truth. But here's the thing: knowing that there were armed guards didn't make me feel safe – it made me feel uneasy. Because they weren't my armed guards, if you know what I mean. I know all the citizen guards by sight. And then there's Geraldine. I didn't know it till I was in the Valley, but I trust her; she makes me feel safe. I'm not saying I didn't feel safe up there, but I was definitely out of my comfort zone.

Anyway, it was a simple deal up in the Valley - if you wanted to eat, you had to earn your food. You could work – milk the goats, clean the barns and hen houses, work in the gardens, join a maintenance team. You could attend classes – understanding Gaia, principles of sustainable agriculture, traditional crafts and skills, world languages, blah, blah, blah. You could explore your creativity through creative writing, healing dance, healing art, 'finding your inner voice', traditional drumming. Or you could do yoga or meditation. Wow, I could hardly contain my excitement! Group meditation, individual meditation, traditional yoga, Bikram yoga, walking meditation. The last one meant you walked around on your own and thought deep thoughts. That appealed to me.

Pippa, of course, signed up for sustainable agriculture, while Planet Boy Damian discovered that traditional skills included archery, so he went off to add that essential life skill to his repertoire.

I decided to wander alone and think deep thoughts that would save the planet and heal the world. Because we all know that if everyone in the world thinks positive thoughts and wants everyone else in the world to be happy, then the psychic energy that will be generated will be so powerful, so positive and so unstoppable that the benefits will be incalculable. Yeah, right.

Anyway, I wandered in the Valley. I climbed up till I could see the two lakes and the whole development. And then I lay back on the turf and let the silence of the place wash over me. There was birdsong – I think it was a thrush, but I'm not sure because the secret life of birds has not featured very highly on my list of essential things that a girl like me needs to know, but it was beautiful.

I'm not sure if I drifted to sleep but after a while I became aware of someone or something close by and I started. I sat up carefully and looked around me. There, not twenty feet away from me, was a red deer, a stag. He stood absolutely still and looked at me. I should have been petrified. Have you ever seen their antlers? There were at least twelve points on his. He could have tossed me in the air for fun. But I wasn't afraid. I was euphoric. He was so beautiful. I wasn't brave enough but I wanted to pet him and climb on his back and ride away like Europa on her white bull.

Then he gave a call that sounded across the valley and he turned without any hurry and moved away. No, I'm not going soft in the head and I haven't lost my critical faculties; I know there's loads of phoniness and mystic crap in the world, but this felt like some kind of sign – a good sign – and I wandered down the hill as bubbly as a bottle of fizzy wine.

That evening we ate in the communal rondavel at tables arranged in concentric circles around the fire.

The food was free from all contamination, totally organic, fresh, vegetarian, good for you (not very tasty or appetising to my meat- and salt-loving palate, but filling) and guaranteed to make you feel a better person. And Damian was totally at home because no one observed the niceties of table manners, which isn't to say they were disgusting, because they weren't, but they lacked finesse.

After supper we sat around and chatted and then a young Pilgrim stepped forward with a guitar and everyone sang old hippy songs: 'We Shall Overcome' and 'Amazing Grace'. By some cool technology the words were projected onto the walls though I couldn't figure out where they came from. It was like a church gathering, which did nothing for me because I was in my agnostic phase, though it wasn't a matter of faith with me. (That's a joke, incidentally. Mattie says I'm the worst teller of jokes ever.)

One thing about the Pilgrims that you need to know: it's not an equal opportunity employer. Who prepared the food? You guessed it: the women. Who served the food and cleared the tables? The women. Who sat at John's feet and gazed with love into his blue eyes? The women. Actually, there were very few women – they were mostly girls, and very pretty they were too.

Did I tell you that John spoke before curfew and everyone went off to bed? Well, he did. I have to hand it to him, he was good. What he said was trite but he spoke with such passion in his voice that every girl there wanted to be his lover and have his babies and take care of him forever, though Gwen would have scratched their eyes out had they even made one little move. Still, I was impressed.

And then it was time to sleep in our little rondavel. Now, let's get this over with: the sleeping arrangements caused me some distress. I mean, I'm the president's daughter. I sleep in my own suite and no one enters without knocking on the door. I'm used to my privacy. Pippa, well, she's a border at our school so that's an end to privacy, and Damian lived like a wild animal so he doesn't care who sees him in what state of undress or hears him peeing. I'm not saying they pranced around in the nude or anything like that, but they got undressed and ready for bed and into their pyjamas without any obvious signs of discomfort. Whereas I went through agonies undressing, putting on my pyjamas, washing my teeth and using the loo (while running the taps) before stepping into my sleeping bag and appearing from my little private space into the rondavel looking like the abominable snowman with a big red face.

The stove sat on a circular platform and you placed your sleeping mats around it with your feet nearest the stove. I lay down, then Pippa got into her sleeping bag and lay on one side of me and Damian got into his and lay on the other. Remember I told you that Pippa had a dog, Moonshine? Well, sometimes I think Pippa is half-dog. I don't mean that as an insult. But she can curl up in her own little world and seem a million miles away and then you mention something of remote interest to her and she's right there in the conversation, fully alert, ready for action. Also, she can sniff out how you're feeling, the way a dog can sense your fear, and take appropriate steps.

Want an example? Well, we turned out the lights and it was dark, I mean dark like the jungle is dark – no, I haven't been to the jungle, but you know what I mean – and I wasn't comfortable because I wasn't used to sleeping with people. I was wondering if I snored or said funny things in my sleep or had nightmares and shouted out 'Mammy'. The whole situation was just a bit freaky and, yes, the rondavel was lovely and snug, but we were sleeping on the floor and I wasn't sure if insects could get in and my scalp felt itchy and I wanted to scratch all over and was sure I'd have to pee again and I wanted to be home in my own bed.

But then Pippa said really quietly, 'Good night, Val,' and she reached out her hand to touch my arm which was up near my head. I stretched out my hand and took hers and that human contact made me feel a whole lot better.

Then Damian touched my other arm and I moved my hand to take his. The reaction was very different and made me think things that I'm not going to tell you but that would have involved me getting out of my sleeping bag and into his. That's all fine in your mind as long as it stays there, but when he said 'Good night, Valentina,' in a soft throaty way, I swear all my insides melted and I didn't trust myself to say a word.

And then they both fell asleep. I didn't because my two arms were stretched out like someone on a rack, but I didn't dare let go and, anyway, the discomfort was worth it because it proved that I was not an alien being, alone and friendless in the world.

Here's a conundrum. You ask me if I slept that night and I'll say no. So how come Damian woke me up and told me breakfast was awaiting me? And, what's more, if I didn't sleep, how come I dreamt of the stag running along the shore of a great ocean, where the waves surged and broke on the land with great force? So, my dear Watson, it's elementary – I did sleep though I have no recollection of so doing because I was … asleep! And I felt refreshed.

Pippa was already up and cleaning our little house – which was spotlessly clean to begin with and hardly needed more cleaning, but there you are – and Damian was looking terrifically pleased with himself and ready to do me any service I required. I felt like a benign queen bee with all her little drones buzzing around.

After I had washed and realised I didn't need two hours to apply make-up and sort out my clothes for the day, I appeared and announced myself ready to have breakfast. This, of course, meant another trip to the communal hall where a delicious (not) breakfast of porridge, fresh fruits and berries, juices (carrot and orange – yuck) soda bread and cheese awaited me, when all I wanted was some nice creamy coffee. Everyone was sister this and brother that so that it might have been a soul music convention.

But most of all it was just fun – fun to be hanging out with Damian and Pippa and fun to be anonymous and to have no responsibility to set the standard as the daughter of the first family, though every time I said to myself, 'This is fun; I have no responsibilities,' the spell broke and I was back to where I started.

Then there was the whole question of why we were there in the first place which, in case you've forgotten, was to establish if you-know-what (the earthquake, the Greenland ice, the flood) had really happened, which was all redundant because I knew it had, even if I wasn't going to admit it to Damian or Pippa.

And there was the related question of whether I was really anonymous or if Mum and Dad had sent their spies to keep an eye on me. Dad had said protection would be 'discreet'. Did that mean Geraldine was traipsing around in the Valley, dressed as a hippy? Yeah, it's tiring being me, in case you hadn't noticed. But that day was pretty cool, all things considered.

I helped in the kitchen with preparing a ginormous

lunch for the community. The chief organiser was a man and all the little helpers were girls but hey, what's new – that's just the way the man bastards run the show. They had these huge pots, straight from the Hansel-and-Gretel-boiling-little-children collection, and we made this chilli con carne, except it was really chilli sin carne but it had all the other ingredients and nearly everything came from their own gardens and greenhouses. Impressive, yeah? Well, I was impressed and I didn't disgrace myself in the kitchen, though it was not exactly my natural habitat. Everyone was laughing and joking and I began to think there might be something to recommend living in a community.

At lunch, Damian and Pippa and I sat together with Joshua close by, and the three people we met on the bus and weirdy Thomas at this great round table. Even though a circle has no beginning or end, it was pretty obvious where the top of the circle was because that's where John and Gwen sat and, whether by accident or design, I was placed so that John and I were sitting directly opposite each other. If I counted the number of times he smiled at me, it would have been embarrassing and it struck me that he was – yes, it's true – very handsome and good-natured, but I still wasn't convinced that he had a brain, though maybe, like the scarecrow, he had a heart.

But I tell you, the chilli sin carne was pretty sensational and as we all slurped it up – OK, OK, I let myself go in the table etiquette department – and listened to the music provided by a Carlos Santana tribute band (that's a whole other story) it was probably one of the happiest moments of my life. Except Mattie wasn't there. If he had been, we would have eaten a midnight feast and told ghost stories, like we used to.

So, did I get a picture of Joshua from that weekend with the Pilgrims? Sort of. I could see he was tall, handsome and strong and looked like he worked out. He was calm, self-possessed, intelligent and observant. He spoke in a very precise way with not a single word wasted and everything he said seemed to be wise and deep. Even when he said ordinary things like 'Pass the bread', it was in such a solemn way that you did it with great reverence. So yeah, you could say I sort of got to know him and I didn't really like him. Though that wouldn't be strictly true. It's just that he was always watching and I wanted to be somewhere where no one was watching.

Anyway, it didn't matter what I thought, because Pippa was smitten with him, head-over-heels, oh my-God-isn't-he-gorgeous smitten, so I reckoned that was enough love and awe for him to be going on with. To be fair to ol' Josh, he behaved like a perfect gentleman towards Pippa. In other words, he didn't take advantage of her innocence and youth or introduce her to the wily ways of the predatory male (I've read the magazines; I know these things). So that was a good mark for Joshua in my book.

But there was just this little something about him. He was too good. Know what I mean? He hung upon the cheek of night like that rich jewel in the Ethiop's ear. Only he was the Ethiop. (*Romeo and Juliet*, Act 1, Scene V. I love that play. We did it at school last year.) But mostly the reason I didn't take to him was because I couldn't figure out what he was thinking, why he was there or whom he served.

Even that oddball weirdo who followed him around, Thomas, who was a right royal pain in the ass, was way easier to read than Joshua. Thomas just served himself. I knew loads of people like that from school. You took one look and you could see through them. Little self-serving shits.

But not Joshua. You looked at him and you saw only darkness. So maybe you could say Joshua frightened me a little bit. But then things happened later and I had a totally different view of him. And of Thomas too, which goes to prove that I can, occasionally, be wrong. (Big of me, eh?)

One thing that didn't happen was that we didn't have a good old heart-to-heart with Joshua about you-know-what and the consequences, which was a blessed relief because I don't think I could have handled all that solemnity. When we said goodbye to John and Gwen and the other Pilgrims and took the minibus back to the tram, I was feeling like a condemned woman who had got a last minute reprieve. Yeah, life's beautiful.

And that feeling stayed with me until we were on the tram, squashed in a seat, when Damian told me, 'Joshua will take us to the Amber Zone in two weeks' time, during the mid-term break.'

I looked round to make sure no one could possibly hear us before saying, 'He's a spy. I know he is. You could be arrested for even wanting to do such a thing.'

'You're right about him being a spy. He works for Solidarity, for your brother.'

If he had slapped me I couldn't have been more surprised, but I tried not to show it and went into a head-down-stare-at-the-floor routine and said nothing, like a prisoner in for interrogation who is determined to show NO EMOTION. After what seemed like ten minutes but was probably only sixty seconds, I said as casually as I could, 'He'll bring us to see Mattie?'

'Yes.'

'Fine.'

I sat back and looked out the window and didn't say another word until we reached the West Shopping Centre. Just as we were about to go our separate ways, I said, 'There's no guarantee my father will allow me to spend mid-term in the Valley.' And for once, Damian didn't make a smart remark.

11

Much to my surprise (and, let's be honest here, disappointment), my father gave me permission to spend the mid-term break in the Pilgrim community, though he repeated the same instructions as before: 'Don't draw attention to yourself.' My heart sank. You know how it is. You're waiting for something to start and you're a nervous wreck. If Mattie had been there, we would have stayed up late and talked it through. But he wasn't.

Some mornings I woke up and felt terrified. The prospect of seeing Mattie should have cheered me. But to sneak out towards the Badlands without all the usual supports that I was now really appreciating – Mum and Dad, Eddie, Geraldine, Francesca, the citizen guards, my phone – filled me with terror. I'm not afraid to admit it: I'm a complete and absolute coward. What the hell was I facing into?

I researched as best I could. And though there were firewalls protecting us from dangerous rumours, there was enough ambiguous information online to make me think that something big was happening out there in the world beyond our borders; something big and bad that I would rather just leave to its own devices. Hey, I'm sure awful things happen in the forests at night, but I'm safe in my bed so I don't really care. Only now the plan was to go into the forest and check out the awful stuff. What kind of plan was that? A plan for crazy people. I wanted to tell Damian it was OK, no further proof required. But sometimes events take on a life of their own and you feel powerless to stop them.

Not that every moment of every day was filled with thoughts of terror and darkness. There was some excitement in school when Sarah Flicker, the head girl, and Jonathan Little, the head boy, were rumoured to have been caught together in the boys' showers in the gymnasium and there were a million, zillion dirty rumours flying about concerning, among other things:

(a) Who was doing what to whom when they were discovered

(b) Who discovered them

(c) Who had reported them

(d) What excuse they made when they were discovered

(e) What state of dress or undress they were in when they where discovered

(f) Where exactly – shower, bench or toilet cubicle – they had been found

(g) What they said when they were discovered – 'Almost done, just another jiffy'?

(h) Whether they had gone 'the whole way'

(i) What their fate would be.

It was a time of delicious rumour and malicious gossip. The only person that I knew for certain knew anything at all was Pippa, who had been in the gym when the offending pair had been escorted to Ms Rumsfeld's office. However, she claimed not to have seen them leave, and the only thing she could remember and would confirm was that she had heard someone talking in the boys' changing rooms, but didn't take much notice of it. Despite all kinds of prompting, Pippa stubbornly refused to allow gossip and a place in school history to overcome her annoying tendency to tell the truth.

The rumours of possible expulsion for Sarah and Jonathan were downright silly. True, the Book forbids sexual relations between young persons before the age of seventeen on the grounds of public morality and health, and equally true, all the students in Thomas Aquinas High School wear chastity rings and take a solemn pledge to refrain from unseemly, unhealthy and immoral sexual activities, and, for the most part, honour their pledge. (As the president's daughter, I am expected to set a standard in this department and, excepting some brief moments of whimsical fantasy in relation to devil-child Damian, I have never found this a burden, given the lamentable absence of anything resembling male beauty in Thomas Aquinas High.)

But even if Little Ms Flicker and Big Mr Little had gone the whole way, they were the head boy and the head girl, from the top hundred families in the Citadel (they were hardly going to make some common girl or boy the head student. After all, what do you think this is – a democracy? Bah, humbug!) and therefore it was inconceivable that they would be found guilty of transgressing the school code and the Book of Rules and receive a public rebuke. Impossible. Unthinkable. Unadmittable.

You might conclude that being the head boy or head girl gave you licence to do anything you liked, because who was going to denounce you? Not true. Because if Little Ms Flicker, who, it must be admitted, had an admirable figure and amazing teeth, and Big Mr Little, who worked out and had bulging muscles and sculpted pecs (which, it was rumoured, he oiled every day) were in fact guilty, nothing would be said in public, but there would be HELL to pay in private. Their families would have to pay out enormous amounts of money to the school and the council to smooth things over. So, even though I knew what the outcome would be, the whole business was a welcome distraction from the prospect of becoming a secret agent and wandering into the Badlands like some teenage pirate queen.

Mr Robert Bowles MA was our history teacher in Thomas Aquinas. We called him Mouldy Old Bowels. He had some disgusting habits, like picking his nose behind his book when he thought no one was looking. Imagine being a teacher, standing every day of your working life in front of twenty young people and labouring under the delusion that a book, which measures approximately eight inches by six, can hide from their prying eyes the sight of a vigorous digital investigation of your nose followed by a visual inspection of the finds made by this examination and then a pathetic attempt to hide the evidence by running the aforementioned digit on the underside of the teacher's desk. Yuck. Such was Mr Bowles. In addition, he was fond of wearing a canary yellow jumper under his brown jacket and he seemed oblivious to the fact that the jumper had a hole in the back of it, as if someone had stubbed out a cigarette on it or him or both.

Intriguingly, Mr Bowles had a wife. By our best estimates, she was twenty years younger than him, tall, glamorous and sexy, and no one could imagine why she had married such a stick insect unless she felt sorry for him or had been sold to him by her poverty-stricken parents. And then there was the speculation that Mr

Bowles was the heir to a vast fortune (I thought this unlikely), which explained his attractiveness to the opposite sex. Now, if there's one word which should not be put with 'Mr Bowles' it is 'sex'. It's just too gross. Which is why, when one of the loud girls asked everyone in the history class to imagine Mr and Mrs Bowles in bed engaging in sexual relations, I had to excuse myself from the room for fifteen minutes at the very idea of such a thing.

Anyway, it was to Mr Bowles that I directed some of the twenty-two thousand and sixty-four questions I had buzzing through my mind on the state of the island. This caused him to experience mild bouts of panic.

Mr Bowles was old school. He talked and you listened. And then he told you to write down some things or underline things in your history book. To do well in history, you were expected to give back to Mr Bowles what he made you write down. He seemed to think that this process ensured some transfer of knowledge from him, the fount of all wisdom, to us, the empty vessels. In other words, Mr Bowles was the Most Boring Teacher Ever. And if that wasn't bad enough, he gave the impression that dealing with fourteen- or fifteen-year-olds was just too much to ask a man of his intellectual accomplishments. In short, Mr Bowles was a creep and a lousy teacher.

Here is a sample of the questions I directed at him:

(a) Was it the influx of immigrants that caused the old government of the island to fall?

(b) How did the Party of Free Citizens gain power?

(c) Was the party right to abandon the west and north of the island?

(d) Was it true that a civil war was raging in the Badlands?

(e) Were the Army of the Tribe criminals or political terrorists?

(f) Could Solidarity be considered an enemy of the State of Free Citizens?

(g) How many people could the island support?

(h) Were the rumours concerning the Greenland icecap true?

(i) If yes, what were the likely consequences for us?

Mouldy Old Bowels generally did not tolerate questions from students and when someone was brave enough to ask one, the response was usually short, sharp and vicious. I had never asked a question because Mr Bowles made the subject so boring that there was never anything that caught my interest. Now, however, there were a hundred things I wanted to discuss. I knew most of the facts, but I wanted to tease out the whys and why-nots of our situation on the island. Not that Bowles was much help. He hummed and hawed and sweated and tried to figure out what I was playing at. Any other student he would have made mincemeat of.

But he knew who I was – everyone knew who I was – and with Geraldine loitering nearby he had to mind his manners. His long, rambling, anxious answers were so qualified and full of 'On the one hand … on the other hand' as to be virtually meaningless but there were a few things he said which I thought interesting, such as:

(a) The actions of the AOT were political, if you call wanting to get rid of every race and colour who were not the original Tribe 'political'.

(b) There were no reports of clashes between Solidarity (Mattie's group) and government forces.

On the climate front, he acknowledged that he had heard the rumours about the Greenland icecap, but he could not say if they were true and suspected they were false, given that they had not been reported in the media.

All the students in the class regarded these exchanges with something approaching awe. None of them had ever seen a student get the better of Mouldy or show impatience when he failed to answer what he had been asked. And no one – I repeat, no one – had ever witnessed him wiping the sweat from his brow. So you could say that I gained a reputation for myself from that little episode. For about two weeks I was a hero for my classmates in history.

Not that I was interested in being a hero. I had maps to study. I wanted to have a mental picture of the place

I was going to. I pored over Damian's map and official maps in our school books. I tried to visualise the unknown land to which I was headed. But all I could see were dark caves and barren mountains and ragged people from distant continents. And everything I imagined was mixed up with stories from childhood of children lost in the forest.

12

So there we were, back up in the Valley, and because we were (ostensibly) staying a week, we were given a Pilgrim scarf and a tunic to wear, which felt a little bit like wearing a school uniform. We were assigned the same rondavel as before, which was cool, though why this should have been important to me is baffling. I suppose it had something to do with security and familiarity and clinging to that kind of stuff before we headed off into God knows where, even as my antennae were taking in everything I could glean about the world beyond our borders.

I was pleased that John was there and even Gwen, who was kind and tried desperately hard to treat me like her little sister, which basically meant talking to me as if I had the intelligence quotient of a newt, which was sweet in a totally annoying kind of way.

But if you ask me, I had no clue as to how we were going to leave the Valley or what plans were in place or who was going to lead us. Joshua was almost invisible, but Thomas resumed paying attention to me so it was pretty much a relief to bed down in our cosy rondavel and snuggle up in my sleeping bag between Pippa and Damian. No, I didn't slip out of my sleeping bag and into anyone else's, nor did anyone slip into mine, because we were in the Circle of Trust and, anyway, the Book of Rules is very clear about that sort of thing.

To tell you the truth, I think Damian was feeling a bit scared himself and worried that his big mouth had gotten us into something that might prove to be a Big Mistake. So he was pretty quiet in himself. I saw this troubled expression on his face that I had not seen before. Maybe I'm making this up after the event, but I seem to remember that in his tunic and scarf, Damian looked small and scared. Pippa, on the other hand, was on high alert like an animal in the wild, fuelled by nervous energy.

On the morning of the third day, as we were leaving the communal rondavel after breakfast, Joshua appeared at my side and I found there was no one else around and he was leading me towards a forest path I had never walked before. I looked around to see if there was anyone else there, but there wasn't. All these crazy ideas tumbled into my mind: what if Joshua was the enemy and wanted to kidnap me and hold me for ransom? What if he intended to murder me? What if Pippa and Damian were in on the scheme? What if this whole thing was a ploy to spirit me away from the Citadel and the Green Zone? What if … What if …

I was looking around trying to figure out a way to escape when Joshua addressed me.

'Miss Valentina, forgive me surprising you in this way, but I need to speak to you on your own.' His tone was so formal and dignified and his words were so soothing that my heart stopped racing and I heard the birds singing and the sound of flowing water. 'Miss Valentina, I need to be sure that you understand the dangers involved in travelling across the Green Zone and further afield. I would not forgive myself if any harm were to befall you. Nor do I believe Matthew would forgive me.'

He paused, waiting for me to reply. I would like to have made some casual-sounding remark about our little adventure and jolly hockey sticks, but I didn't because, even though my heart was calm and I was now certain that Joshua had no ulterior motive in bringing me into the forest, my brain was still intact and prevented me from presenting a cheerful and smiling face to the world.

I knew about our island. But knowing about something and knowing something are two quite different matters. The research I had done in the last few weeks had filled me with dread. I knew that people were dying every day somewhere in the world, which was remote and unreal, but this wasn't 'somewhere in the world' – this was my island. I couldn't stop thinking of Mattie and Solidarity and the fights that had been reported between them and the AOT.

I had this image in my head that I couldn't shake off. It was a young man spread-eagled on the ground where the AOT had murdered him and they stood around smiling, holding their machine guns as they mugged for the camera. Even though I couldn't see the victim's face I could see the soles of his bare feet and I feared if I got nearer I would recognise him. So no, I didn't pretend that this was all just an awfully big adventure, like something out of the Famous Five.

Joshua continued but I was only half-listening because I was still trying to find a way of sneaking up on to the imaginary dead body to see if it was Mattie. But I heard enough of what he said about the Badlands: the great river, thick with the blood of the slaughtered; the countryside filled with diseased and dying people; the marauding gangs; the breakdown of law and order. It made me feel sick. But I wasn't going to let him or anyone else see that. And then he stood directly in my line of sight so that I had to give him my full attention.

'Perhaps it would be better if you stayed, Miss Valentina. You do not have to subject yourself to danger. I will be happy to carry any letter or message you wish to pass on to Matthew. And I will report to you all that I learn of the situation in the Western Province and in the Badlands beyond, following the recent event in Greenland.'

He paused and I could tell he was trying to gauge my reaction. I knew by the way he was looking at me that he couldn't figure out what was going on in my head. That pleased me because it proved that I was developing my own air of inscrutability in the best tradition of my mother and father. And then he reached into his tunic and produced an envelope.

'Matthew asked me to give this to you.'

I took the envelope and put it into the back pocket of my jeans without even looking at it. Then I said very slowly and deliberately, 'I will go.'

Joshua nodded and moved quickly to brief me on the plans. We'd be leaving just before dawn the following morning. He was still speaking in a dignified way but he was talking faster now and was itemising everything I should bring and how I should dress and what kind of shoes I'd need. He went over everything twice and when I asked him how we would explain our disappearance to John he told me that John had given him permission to take us on a forty-eight-hour adventure trip in the mountains to develop our wilderness skills, which was a regular feature of community activities.

At that moment I would love to have had a consult-a-friend option. And the friend I'd have chosen was my father. But I didn't, of course. And before I knew it, we were back at the communal rondavel and Joshua had slipped away.

So this was it. There was no going back. I had chosen. I didn't feel brave. In fact, I marvelled at myself for refusing the pass card that Joshua had offered me. I'm not sure I can explain why I refused, though I think it had to do with Mattie, which was only to be expected, and in some other less clear way, with my father, which was something of a surprise. I didn't want to let him down. Only then did I take out the envelope and read Mattie's note:

Hello Sis. It would be lovely to see you. But I'll understand if you don't come. You can trust J. Do everything he tells you. Love, M.

I wandered around a track that was used for walking meditation and read the words over and over. It would be lovely to see you. It would be lovely to see you. It would be lovely to see you. Round and round. Over and over.

That night in our rondavel, we prepared for the morning. We were very quiet. We packed our rucksacks and made sure we had warm clothes – I had Mattie's sweater – and good shoes to wear. Then we got ready for bed and settled down in what was an almost familiar pattern – me lying between Pippa and Damian. It was really dark and silent in the rondavel; I could sense every little movement of the other two and I knew they were as wide awake as I was, though nobody said a word. And then Pippa slid her hand over towards me and found mine and we each held tight and before long I was holding Damian's hand too. I kept asking myself why I was going on this stupid trip. And myself had little to say in reply. But I kept talking anyway.

Me: This is going to be different from anything you've known or want to know. So why are you going?

Myself: You know the answer to that.

Me: It would be lovely to see you. And it would be lovely to die, too, I suppose?

Myself: Shut up and leave me alone.

Me: It's not going to be fun, you know. There are no shopping centres in the big bad world and you won't have your chauffeur-driven car to bring you here and there for all your little appointments. Or maybe you think your Damian is going to turn into a hero and rescue you if things go wrong?

Myself: Go away.

Me: Why are you putting yourself in danger? Because the one-time wild child got under your skin? Because you think you have feelings for him? How pathetic is that?'

Myself: I've stopped listening.

Me: What good will it do the poor people who live in the Badlands if you catch a glimpse of how they live?

Myself: Maybe because I want to see for myself what their life is like.

Me: Oh, yeah? You want to be a poverty tourist? 'Oh my God, look over there! Where's my camera?'

Myself: Piss off.

Me: Or maybe it's decaying corpses you're after, with your shiny little camera?

Myself: Are you still here?

Me: You might get lucky and witness the AOT in action.

Myself: I need to know why Mattie left and why he hasn't come back. OK? Happy now? Happy you have me crying? Leave me alone.

The feeling that had been building up inside me burst out and I began to sob as if I was the loneliest, saddest person on the planet. Damian and Pippa tried to put their arms around me to comfort me. Have you ever tried to put your arms around someone when you're trapped in a sleeping bag? It's not the easiest thing in the world to do and I was more squashed than hugged and in the end my sobs turned to laughter, and we eventually fell asleep in a tangled heap of sleeping bags, elbows and hands.

It would be great to be able to report that after my dark night of the soul, I woke up refreshed and ready to face the world with renewed energy and joy in my heart. But I didn't. And here's why.

First of all, I didn't wake. I was woken by Joshua knocking on the door and coming in at what seemed like the middle of the night. Secondly, I felt wrecked, totally wiped. And thirdly, Thomas was with Joshua and his eyes were on me from the moment I managed to drag myself upright and open my eyes. And though I may be possibly the most beautiful girl on the planet (apart from the lovely Pippa, of course), I didn't want a pair of hungry eyes on me, eating me up at that hour of the day.

Joshua shushed us and put his fingers to his mouth until I wanted to slap his hand and tell him to push his shushes up his you-know-where and let me go back to sleep. Damian and Pippa had the good sense to stay clear of me and mind their own business, which was, under the circumstances, wise of them. We had our jackets and scarves on and our rucksacks on our backs and we crept out and took a path away from the central buildings till we came to a shed that must have belonged to the farm which was here before the Pilgrims moved in.

Stage one of the great big adventure: creep to a cowhouse – brilliant. In the shed, there was an old Land Rover and Joshua signalled to us to put our rucksacks in the back and get in.

He started the engine and we were away, driving slowly with no lights on up the valley towards the ridge which led into the mountains. If there were guards, none stopped us and I knew better than to ask too many questions because the less people knew about the arrangements, the safer for all of us. And though I wasn't sure I liked Joshua, I trusted Mattie and trusted that things had been well planned, which is not to say that things went smoothly, because, frankly, they didn't.

As you may have guessed, travelling in the back of a Land Rover over a mountain was a new experience for me. Not a pleasant experience, but a new one. And soon, very soon, I felt as sick as a dog. And soon after that, I was as sick as a dog, throwing up the multi-coloured contents of my stomach on the mountainside, surrounded by a concerned audience of four. Wonderful. In one of those surreal moments of insight that comes while you are puking up your guts, I realised that vegetable soup and puking seemed indelibly intertwined in my life. And, as an addendum, I wondered if Damian was staring at my ass. (If he was, I felt entitled to be mad; if he wasn't, I felt equally entitled to be mad.) When, at last, it seemed that I had evacuated my stomach, I felt Joshua's hand on my back.

'Are you feeling better now, Miss Valentina?' he asked and I thought this probably the most stupid question I had ever been asked. How did he think I was feeling?

'I'm fine,' I answered with my fixed smile in place, 'absolutely fine.' And to prove this true, I began to get to my feet with an air of perfect confidence only to be racked by another spasm. What little liquid was left inside me spurted out, narrowly missing Thomas. How smooth was that? This time, though, I did make it to the upright position and, mustering what authority I could command, announced that we really should get going.

Joshua handed me a bottle of water and I poured some on my hands, rubbed the back of my neck, splashed my face and drank a little, and the three others gave me the kind of looks that made me want to throw up all over again.

'It will be easier if you sit in the front,' Joshua said.

I didn't argue but got straight into the Land Rover as if nothing had happened, quite prepared to face any danger that might befall us. (Though inwardly I knew I sucked at being an action hero.)

At this point, I wish I could relate some dangerous adventure that did befall us, or a growing sense of danger and threat, a darkening of the sky, an unshakeable feeling of foreboding. The truth is that for the rest of the morning we drove leisurely across the mountains, where the only living things we saw were some sheep and a herd of wild ponies who showed not the slightest interest in us as they grazed away to their hearts' content. High in the mountains, the world was de-cluttered and all the stuff that surrounded me and that I had known for fourteen years seemed to belong to a different place. Here there were no parents, no teachers, no jocks, no queen bees, no uniforms, no roads, no timetables – none of the things that made my world what it is. Here you could make up a new world, start from scratch. That, I suppose, was what the Pilgrims were supposed to be doing a couple of miles away in the next valley, except that their attempts at making a new world were a bit superficial.

From the position of the sun, I figured out that we were heading in a south-westerly direction. (Surprising, perhaps, but I have my orienteering badges from the Girl Guides, though I admit it's unbelievable that anything from that sad chapter in my life actually came in useful.)

Anyway, we were going through the most deserted countryside I'd ever seen. There was no one there. It wasn't barren, it was just empty. Places that are completely empty are beautiful and lonely and sad and calming. There were still little streams that we crossed, and clumps of yellow gorse in bloom and pockets of purple heather which were really pretty. It was hard to imagine that somewhere else on the island, people were living on top of each other and the land was flooded. Why didn't some of them move up here? (But I knew the answer to that question before I even asked it: this was our land and we didn't want a raggle-taggle rabble moving in and spoiling it.)

In the middle of the morning, we stopped and ate the food that Thomas had brought for us all. There was fruit and nuts and seeds and fresh milk and some hard-boiled eggs. We spread a groundsheet on the banks of a stream and sat in the shelter of a big boulder. By now the car sickness was well and truly gone and I felt famished. We had no cutlery so we all ate with our fingers and Damian's table manners seemed a lot less disgusting in this company.

'The countryside reminds me of Norway,' Pippa said. She wasn't sad or anything – it was just a statement of fact.

'Parts of the Ethiopian highlands are like this too,'

Joshua said, which was news to me because I thought most of that part of the world was desert but I didn't say anything because I wasn't going to parade my ignorance.

'And the Masa Marai,' Thomas said. But I didn't believe him because that's Kenya and they have or used to have lions and elephants and rhinos and stuff and there's no way in the wide earthly world that the mountains around the Citadel are where you'd find those kinds of animals, so I reckoned he was just saying that to fit in. I might have smiled sweetly at him, only that would have encouraged him and he was bad enough as things were. I swear, at any moment I was expecting him to start licking me like some ridiculously annoying dog. So I was glad when Joshua told us it was time to get going because we had to make our rendezvous point by late afternoon.

I bit my lip. If the opportunity arose, I'd speak to Joshua alone. But I didn't want to ask idle questions that might put us or Mattie in danger. So I didn't ask where the rendezvous point was and if we'd meet Mattie there. If we were to meet Mattie, then we must be crossing into the Amber Zone with him because there was no way we were going to be out of the Green Zone by mid-afternoon. Nor did I ask why we had encountered no guards as we left the camp or if there were guards patrolling these mountains and, if so, what we would do if we encountered them. No, I kept my questions to myself.

I didn't give myself much time to consider why I was being so cautious. Now, of course, I know the answer to that and will admit it: I was cautious because it was second nature to me. I was my parents' daughter. It wasn't that I didn't trust my companions; I did. But that didn't mean I was going to change who I was.

We continued as before, keeping off roads and travelling across open country till the scenery began to change. It was still pretty wild, but here and there were abandoned houses and a few ruins and stone walls and enclosures. In one place there was a deserted village. The houses might have been two hundred years old or even older. It was Thomas who called to Joshua that there was someone moving around one of them. Joshua told everyone to behave as normal and then he asked Thomas to describe exactly what he had seen. (Why do people say 'Behave as if nothing has happened' in situations where the only thing you are sure of is that something has happened and you're nervous?)

'An old boy,' Thomas was saying, 'moving on shaky legs, like a stork's.'

'Just one?'

'Yes.'

'Near the last house on the right?'

'Yes.'

'I'm going to stop the jeep. You must all stay here,' Joshua said and he looked particularly at me, as if I was going to jump out of the jeep and lead the Charge of the Light Brigade.

'Thomas, come and sit in the driver's seat,' Joshua ordered. 'If anything happens, you drive away and head back to the community. You understand?'

'Yes, sir.'

That was a really helpful thing to say.

Have you ever thought about the sound of fear? I hadn't until that moment. But then I heard it in the silence – the sound of fear is when no one makes a sound.

Joshua took his long stick and I saw him pat his tunic where I knew he carried his knife and maybe a gun. Maybe Ethiopian princes have special issue Uzi machine guns. I don't know.

We watched with our hearts in our mouths as he walked towards the ruin. He called out a greeting in a language I didn't understand. As he got nearer, a man came from the side of the house. He was not old but he looked weak and unwell. He held a machete and raised it to signal to Joshua to stop.

The man looked so pathetic that I wanted to laugh, which is, I guess, a relief mechanism. Still, a machete is a machete, so Joshua stood where he was and spoke calmly. It must have been the correct language because the man answered and Joshua spoke some more and the man pointed towards the old house.

The woman who stood in the doorway seemed to have materialised out of thin air. I nearly died of fright when I saw her. She was tall and might have been beautiful once, but now looked sick and on the point of collapse. From behind her, two pairs of eyes peeked out, like bush babies in the forest at night. I realised that if we were afraid then these people were scared out of their minds.

Joshua nodded and spoke again to the man, who dropped his machete and went to the woman and children.

Joshua came back to the jeep.

'Who are they?' I asked. 'Are they all right? Can I help?'

'Please, Miss Valentina, you stay in the jeep. I will offer what assistance I can.'

'I can help you,' I said, irritated at being dismissed, and it was this, rather than any desire to be a girl guide, that inspired me.

'No. They may be contaminated. It's best if all of you stay.' Joshua had that this-is-very-serious-business-that-only-a-man-can-attend-to expression which made me:

(a) want to laugh

(b) want to punch him in the head

(c) want to make a speech on men and their

ridiculous way of thinking that they are always the ones to solve problems or take the lead in a time of crisis.

All of these options I turned over in my mind as I watched him take a pot and a knife from the provisions he had brought and return to the family. He disappeared into the ruined house. When one of the children wandered out alone and stood looking in our direction, I ignored Joshua's instructions, got out of the jeep and went towards the child. I'm no Mother Teresa of Calcutta or Florence Nightingale, but here was this little black kid wandering around in the middle of nowhere looking so sad that I just did what seemed the most natural thing in the world – I held out my arms and the little boy reached out to me and I lifted him up and held him.

Now, let's get this straight: I'm not the maternal kind. I've no desire to bring twenty babies, or even one, into this world. Also, I'm not into other people's kids and gooing at them and talking in that ridiculousway that adults have when they speak to toddlers, as if children were mentally deficient. OK? Is that clear? But something happened when that little boy wrapped his arms and his legs around me and snuggled into me. I closed my eyes and just stood there holding him, swaying to some inner rhythm I didn't even know I had.

I brought the little boy over to the jeep to get some

water. And guess what? Thomas got all agitated and started shaking his head and waving me away.

'No, Miss Valentina. This is not a good idea.'

'Just hand me a bottle of water,' I said in my hissing queen bee voice, because he really peed me off, acting like this little boy was leaking poison and disease.

And then my one-time hero, the boy I thought about in bed at night, joined in. 'Thomas is right,' Damian said. 'The kid is sick. You don't know what he has.'

'Well, God help me if I catch what you have,' I said, my feelings for Damian disappearing down a virtual toilet. 'Just give me the water.'

Thomas did as I ordered him and I went back towards the house. I sat with my back against the gable and played Mammy and indulged in some comforting boy-hating, which is always good for the soul.

Pippa came and sat beside me. I didn't say anything to her. But I was glad she came because we formed a confederacy of free girls against fearful, selfish, annoying and cowardly boys. We stayed there with our little boy until Joshua appeared. I knew by the look on his face what he was thinking: there was no telling if we had been exposed to some infectious or contagious disease, some terrible affliction normally confined to tropical countries.

'Will they be OK?'

'I will arrange for the border guards to come tomorrow.'

'Where will they be taken?'

'To a quarantine centre.' He held out his arms for the child.

When my little friend realised I was going to pass him over, he held tight and put his head into my shoulder and I swear I wanted to hold on to him even though I knew he had to go back to his mother.

It was Pippa who helped to free me from the boy's grip before Joshua returned him to his family.

Back in the jeep, I listened in silence as Joshua told me the family's story. They came from West Africa. They had sold all their possessions to pay a smuggler to bring them to the island. A guide had led them here and promised they would be collected in twenty-four hours. That was a week ago. They had no food. They'd found potatoes but with no fire and no way to cook them, ate them raw.

'What's a quarantine centre?'

'All illegal immigrants found in the Amber or Green Zones are brought there to be decontaminated.'

I didn't need to hear any more. In fact I stopped listening to what Joshua was saying because I was imagining what he wasn't telling me and would never tell me: how men, women and children were separated in the quarantine centre (believe me, they'd do that for sure); how hard and impersonal the regime was; how the immigrants who survived were sent back to where they came from. I was thinking of the diseases that

I heard mentioned in our moral education and social awareness class, all those D-words and T-words: typhoid, tetanus, tuberculosis, diphtheria, dysentery, diarrhoea and random stuff like malaria and rabies, all of which make you sick, really sick, disgustingly sick, not to mention giving you rashes and sores all over.

I was probably the most immunised person on the whole island (my parents were obsessive about health), but how protected was this little boy and his family? Just think about it. How do you pick up most diseases? By shaking hands, by sneezing, by kissing, by physical contact, by having sex, from insects, from fleas, from stagnant water, from dogs or cats, from infected air. So how do you defend yourself from disease and fever if you don't live in the most medically sanitised state on the planet? Well, you can't – unless, that is, you don't breathe or touch or drink or live. That's how it is in the Badlands. If you want to be sure that you don't pick up some horrible disease, just die. Brilliant, isn't it?

So this was it. This was what I was supposed to be doing? Sucking it up. Learning what life in the big bad world was really like. Only I already knew what it was like. But the little voice in my head countered that: maybe you know what life is like but now you are finally facing up to it.

I sat in the front of the jeep and disappeared into myself. I didn't want to be with Damian who had goaded me into this trip and who now sat on the back seat looking small and insignificant and who wouldn't help a little boy because he might have been sick. At that moment, my love affair with Damian was over. I was angry with Joshua too because of the things he knew and wouldn't say. And I was thoroughly fed up with the ever-watchful Thomas.

So that left Pippa. I didn't have to look over my shoulder to know that she had entered into one of her states of suspended animation. Maybe that's because she came from the far north. I read somewhere that people who live near the Arctic learn how to flatline so that they won't die in the freezing temperatures, or something like that. If we could have magicked ourselves to my room in my house, we would have sat with our arms around each other without saying a word. Except there was no magic and we were stuck in a jeep heading further away from where I wanted to be at that moment.

OK, OK, I know I sound a bit mixed up. Well, that's because I was a bit mixed up. One minute I thought I was in love with Damian and my body thrilled to be close to him; other times I thought him ridiculously young and immature and wondered how I could possibly have imagined myself in love with him.

And because I was more inclined to think of him as ridiculously young on that afternoon, it seemed right to be sitting in the front of the jeep with Joshua, separate from the children in the back. I was making cases to myself why I should never think of him in a positive light when, of course, I'd argue against myself and sneak a look at him in the back and then I'd become irritated with myself for being so weak and start the thinking process all over again. These kinds of thoughts and the see-saw emotions they give rise to afflicted me for most of the afternoon as we travelled west towards the border of the Green and Amber Zones at the River Nore.

We were no longer in mountainous country so it was impossible to keep off the roads because the land was cultivated and there were hedges and ditches and fenced and gated fields and while our Land Rover was an off-road vehicle, it wasn't Chitty Chitty Bang Bang, so it couldn't exactly fly or jump over locked gates.

So we kept off the main roads, going as stealthily as possible along the windy, narrow back roads. But even on these little roads, it was impossible to stay unnoticed because there were farmhouses, lots of them, and people out and about in fields and farmyards. We even passed through small clusters of townlands which had the best names of anywhere in the world, like Pelttown or Palatine. And there was Pollerton, Strawhall and Rathnapish. Pity the poor girl who had to give her address as 'Rathnapish'.

But do you know what struck me most as we travelled along, apart from the side-splitting names? The fact that life there was normal. If people saw us drive by, they looked in our direction and smiled or waved or both. What century did these people belong to? Didn't they know about the sickness and the floods and the immigrants and the AOT? What state of denial were they in?

The second thing that struck my fantastic

journalistic brain (I could imagine myself reporting on the TV news channel) was that everything, and I mean everything, was as neat and ordered as could be and nothing was out of place. Nothing. Just like at home. Because, of course, this was the Green Zone, the State of Free Citizens, where I come from. But I didn't want to expend the mental energy to make the connection between them and me, the connection between their denial and my denial, or the pretty obvious connection between an obsession with order and a refusal to confront the mess and confusion a few hours away. All that stuff was too hard. Better by far to keep your head down and your garden tidy. No, I didn't want to make the effort; I just wanted to go shopping. I just wanted to buy a pair of beautiful shoes. I just wanted to bury my head in the sand, be shallow and tiresome and clichéd.

Mental note to self: It is hard to bury your head in the sand when you begin to encounter armoured vehicles and armed soldiers on the roads and helicopters circling overhead. To do that you'd need an awful lot of sand or a very small head, neither of which I possessed.

And then came the checkpoint. I was worried as we approached it (I never claimed to be hero material), even though these were border guards and on our side and we were still in the Green Zone. Well, it may have been the Green Zone but I was way out of my comfort zone and we could have been in Honolulu for all I recognised of the countryside. It wasn't like the checkpoints they sometimes mount in the Citadel, where bored, pretty boys go through the motions of checking your bag but are really just trying to be cool and flirt with you in a passive-aggressive kind of way, and all the girls swoon: 'OMG, all the pretty boys.'

But these guys weren't playing at being soldiers – they were the real thing. That was scary. Then I was worried in case I'd be recognised. However, once the soldier in charge spoke to Joshua and inspected his papers, the tension disappeared from the air and he showed no interest in the passengers in the car. We were not-very-important-people in the capable hands of a very-important-person which meant we were in the category of people you didn't have to bother about (which, let's face it, is a bit of a let-down). So, on that see-saw afternoon, I flipped from being worried about being recognised to disappointment that I wasn't being recognised. I am a shallow, shallow girl.

Then Joshua got out of the jeep and was introduced to an officer sort and spoke quietly for a few minutes and when he came back to the jeep he looked vexed or worried or both.

'There's been trouble in the Amber Zone, across the border from here. The AOT were spotted in the area. The border guards are searching for them now, so it's not safe for us to cross today. We'll have to wait till morning.'

'Till morning!' I cried. 'No way. You can't tell me that I can't see Mattie. He'll be waiting.'

'If Matthew could guarantee your safety, we'd go; otherwise we stay. There is no argument, Miss Valentina. There's a safe place we can stay.'

There is no argument, Miss Valentina. I did a pretty good impression of Joshua (in my head – I'm not that stupid). I wanted to scream and shout and say no way were some random AOT group going to stop me from seeing Mattie. But I realised that would have been a futile thing to do because, like it or lump it, I was not the queen bee when it came to Joshua.

So I did the next best thing. I sulked, which was probably the sort of behaviour that belonged to the back of the jeep, but who ever claimed that my behaviour was consistently mature? Not me.

About a mile or two down the road, we came to a watchtower which was flying the State of Free Citizens flag (white with a ring of green stars) and had border guards on duty. We turned in at an entrance.

When the sentries waved us through we entered a pretty spectacular tree-lined avenue, if you like that sort of thing. (And do I like that sort of thing? Yes, I do.) The trees, for starters, were real trees – old and gnarled and BIG, like oak or beech. I could have asked Pippa, the expert on all things leaved and blooming, but I was enjoying my queenly position in the front of the jeep and didn't want to submit to anyone else's superior knowledge.

After a leisurely drive – I could practically see the horses and carriages making their stately way up the avenue – we turned into the forecourt of Sandybrook House. That's what it was called, though I didn't know that at the time. It had seen better days and there was a general air of things falling into disrepair and neglect, but it was still a beautiful house, made all the more beautiful by the late-blooming flowers and the grasses that grew around it like a wild meadow. Chickens scratched in the gravel and three big dogs lolled about. It was just the kind of place where llamas and alpacas might turn up, and black pigs and angora rabbits. It was pretty damn cool and so unexpected, so unbelievably unexpected. There were granite steps to the front door and three windows on each side and three storeys over the basement. For me it was love at first sight. I looked at Pippa and smiled. I knew she got it too.

There was no one to greet us. Since the front door was ajar and the ancient doorbell made no sound, we went into the hall, though it felt like trespassing to do so. The hall was large and the stairs rose from the centre. On the landing was a high window that looked over the fields and meadows. Inside, the house was in good enough repair, though there was very little furniture, and it felt as if the occupants were in the process of moving in or moving out.

The five of us stood there and no one spoke until Pippa whispered, 'Will I try to find someone?'

Before I could answer, we heard voices from somewhere above us, and a woman laughing in a way that sounded unnatural.

The whole thing was a little freaky and I was beginning to wonder who, if anyone, lived here when a woman appeared at the top of the stairs and said, 'Oh, you've arrived. We didn't think you'd be here so soon,' in a voice which was a little posh, in an old-fashioned way. On first impression, she didn't seem like the kind of person who would boil children in pots or abandon you in the woods or feed you poison apples. But then you never can tell, can you?

She came down the stairs and shook everyone's hand in a hearty, no-nonsense kind of way and introduced herself as Cordelia, which I thought a pretty cool name, but she was nothing like what a Cordelia should look like, which is young, beautiful and whimsical. This Cordelia was middle-aged and large and wore a faded blue summer dress that might have been made out of a pair of old curtains.

She gave us a little speech on the family as if we were a group of tourists come for a tour: the house was Sandybrook House; the family were the Devereuxes She lived here with her younger sister, who wasn't well (stark raving mad is what she meant, but we figured that out pretty quickly), and her mother, who was getting on a bit (also mad, but not as far gone as her daughter) but a lovely soul. (They were all lovely souls in a funny, sad way.)

Halfway through her little speech, she ran out of steam and began to look through us as if there was something in the distance that commanded all her attention and we were preventing her from going in pursuit of it. It was all a bit weird. She concluded by telling us that the family had another house, a much finer house, in Tipperary, which was now in the Amber Zone, but they had been forced to abandon it after they'd been raided by a gang of criminals and terrible atrocities had been committed against the family.

I had just about had enough when Cordelia turned and signalled to us to follow her up the staircase. Two corridors ran off the first landing, one to the right and one to the left.

'Ladies, this way,' Cordelia said and she showed Pippa and me to our room.

Joshua, Thomas and Damian were given a room on the other side of the staircase – so there was to be no hanky panky between the ladies and the gentlemen in Sandybrook House if Cordelia – Miss Devereux – was going to have anything to do with it. Which was fine by me, because Damian had disappeared so far into himself by this time that there was nothing to love. He was a coat with no one inside.

That's not to say that Pippa and I didn't go to look at the boys' room and compare it with our own. We did that almost immediately and they were pretty similar. Theirs looked over the farmyard with its ancient stone buildings and rusting tractors and farm machines. Beyond the yard you could make out a walled garden and what must have been an orchard an eternity ago. Beyond that was a parkland with old trees still hanging on to their leaves and crows' nests. Pippa looked out the window and I could see her mind whirring as she restocked the orchard and cut back the old trees.

Our room looked out onto the front avenue and the fields where cows must once have grazed and crops grown. It was an enormous room with a wooden floor, the boards of which were two feet wide and worn smooth and dark with age. The windows were high and hung with old velvet curtains that might once have been red but were now bleached a faded brown, like the colour of dried blood. The fireplace was an old marble thing – not grand and arty but cold and black and forbidding. The walls were covered in what at first I thought was faded golden wallpaper but which turned out to be paint with stencil designs of garlands and leaves. It had to be a hundred years old but it looked pretty darn good for its age. There was one enormous four-poster bed whose springs seemed shot – the mattress sagged in the middle – and I wondered who had cavorted so strenuously as to break the back of the bed. The only other things in the room, which was half the size of a football pitch, were an old desk and a single wooden chair. We loved it. Pippa walked around slowly and touched every surface and nodded her approval.

Do you believe in possession? That spirits can take hold of your soul? I know it's a bit weird, but I did feel possessed in Sandybrook. I'm serious. No, the spirit of a dead child didn't take hold of me nor did I start speaking in tongues in a high-pitched little voice, but something happened there, in that strange, beautiful house.

Pippa said she wanted to look at the orchard and off she went. I took a nap because I suddenly remembered how exhausted I was; how long I'd been awake; how badly I'd slept the night before; how tense I'd been all day; how awful I felt about the little boy and his family, abandoned in the deserted village. When I saw that big sagging bed, I just climbed on it and fell fast asleep. But sleeping there in that cavernous room was like falling into the mind of the building itself. I know that sounds weird but that's what it felt like.

When I woke later and went downstairs, I met the old mother, Mrs Devereaux. She was grey-haired and wild-eyed and went wandering around the house putting wild flowers into old vases, jamjars, bottles – anything she could lay her hands on. Some of the flowers gave off a disgusting smell, like cats' pee, but she didn't notice. And she never changed the water, so the whole house had this unsettling smell leaking out from every corner. Though there were enough cats wandering around to make that smell all on their own.

Not that Cordelia did much better. She spent

her time knitting hats and scarves for the soldiers who were billeted in what she told us had been the land steward's house when the family had wealth and influence. Only, when we were there, she wasn't satisfied with her efforts so she ripped everything she had done and started over. I suspected that was what happened every day: every morning she'd begin a grey scarf; every evening she'd rip it apart. How sad and messed up do you have to be to behave like that?

And then there was Daisy, the younger of the two sisters, even if she was at least forty. She wandered around in a gold dress that hugged her body and wore a boa feather and a little hat and puffed on an empty cigarette holder.

'Hello, darling,' she said to everyone and invited each of the boys – Joshua, Thomas and Damian – to her room for 'fun and games' and then she laughed hysterically. Which was why the boys more or less disappeared from Sandybrook while we were there and spent their time at the land steward's house with the border guards, so that Sandybrook was really a women's house, which was fine by me.

Pippa and I wondered if any of the border guards accepted her invitation and if they did, what happened in her room on the third floor? Or was her life as lonely and as deranged as I suspected it was and did she lie on her little bed (that's how I imagined it, a little bed, in a nursery room) pretending she was being loved?

In normal circumstances I would have thought these three women completely batty, but I didn't because I felt so much at home there. And Pippa felt the same way.

The boys were nowhere to be found, having been
frightened off, like I said, by Daisy and Mrs Devereux,
so Pippa and I did a little bit of exploring in the old
house. In the hallway and the drawing room (a great
big room, with just three armchairs marooned in the
middle) there were a few framed photos of Cordelia,
Daisy, their mother, a man I took to be the girls' father
and another I took to be their brother.

What terrible thing had happened to them to make
them all as mad and hopeless as they were? I knew
what they were doing. I got it. They wanted to pretend
that things were as they had been some time in the past,
twenty years ago, when they lived a normal life, when
they had dinner parties and the young ladies dressed
and drank a little too much and got tipsy and flirted
with the male guests, and Mrs Devereaux filled the

house with flowers and everyone said the Devereauxes were the luckiest family on the island. Cordelia had a secret lover who was in the army and she knitted him scarves like they did in the last century, when the 'boys' were away fighting The Enemy; she sent it to him as the kind of playful present that young women in love send to young men and she dreamed that when he came home they would marry and live in a house like this one, Sandybrook House, and make beautiful babies by breaking the springs of big four-poster beds and the babies would grow into little girls who would have ponies and would pester them to give parties.

So what had happened? What terrible thing had robbed them of their dream? Why were they living like people who were exiles from their own lives? That's what they were: exiles, immigrants, stuck in a strange place that wasn't really home.

Later that evening, Cordelia found me and Pippa wandering and insisted we come to the kitchen for tea and scones, which sounded good to me (and I was pretty sure that the table manners in Sandybrook House would be first class). Pretty soon, we were sitting at the big deal table, all snug and cosy with the range burning and feeling totally at ease with this woman whom we'd only met for the first time a few hours before. That's when Cordelia told us what had happened to them.

They had been living in their other house, their real family home (though I thought Sandybrook was about as perfect a family home as you could imagine). The new state had come into existence and their house was not within the Green Zone.

At first they weren't worried. All the madness was happening in the Western Province. But then bands of young men, wild and criminal, began making raids across the river from the Badlands. The family pleaded with the government for more protection but they were told they'd have to move to the Green Zone, to Sandybrook House, if they wanted to be one hundred per cent sure of protection. They debated and delayed until it was too late.

A gang of lawless young men made a raid on the district and, as theirs was the biggest estate around, the family was targeted. At first the attackers overran the farm and set fire to hay barns and looted the outbuildings. Cordelia's father, Major Devereaux, a retired British Army officer; her brother Will, who was only twenty; and Robert, the army officer she loved, who was visiting the family, loaded the family's hunting rifles and went off to confront the raiders and drive them off.

But the gang was much bigger than they'd expected. There was a confrontation and one of the gang members was shot and killed. Then all hell broke loose and the raiders went berserk. Cordelia didn't lay it out too clearly. But she said enough to make us understand that the gang had burst into the house, high on killing and drugs. Daisy had been taken away and raped; their father, brother and the young man she'd hoped to marry were killed in front of her mother. She didn't say what had happened to her and I didn't ask.

Nowadays, the army, our army, paid a small rent for leasing the steward's house and made minor repairs to the building, which, touch wood, was holding up pretty well. At this point she paused. I looked over to Pippa, who was crying silent tears and I guess she was thinking about her family and whether they were all right and if the same kind of terrible things could happen to them. As I was trying hard not to think too much about what Cordelia had told us, she said something that startled me.

'You have no idea what your visit means to us.'

What my visit meant to them? Who did they think I was? And as if she'd read my mind, she continued, 'Your father is a great man.'

'Thank you,' I said with perfect good manners, as I'd been trained to. But all the while my little brain was whirling, like a helicopter. How did Cordelia know who I was? And who the hell was I anyway? I smiled my fixed smile. 'Thank you.'

'The rumours have been flying that you were planning to visit. I didn't pay heed to them. It's better not to get one's hopes up. And then you came.'

This was a pretty nice little speech and if she'd left it at that I wouldn't have been so freaked.

But she didn't. Instead, she came to my side of the table and went down on her knees and took my hand and kissed it and cried. A grown woman who had managed to survive what she had survived and was now keeping her family alive was on her knees, kissing my hand. They didn't teach you the rules for that in the courtesy class in Thomas Aquinas High School.

I didn't know what was going on, but somehow I kept calm. I didn't pull my hand away. And when she put her head on my lap, I stroked her hair over and over and soothed her until the crying stopped. As soon as we could do so without being rude, Pippa and I took our leave and wished her good night.

When we were safe in our room, I said to Pippa, 'What was all that about?'

'You are loved, Val.'

'That's ridiculous.'

'People respect your father but they fear him. They need to believe in someone whom they can love and admire – and you're the one.'

'But they don't know me or anything about me.'

'They don't have to. They're in love with the idea of you. Your father is the stern king and you're the gentle princess. You're their fairytale, Val.'

Lying in my broken four-poster bed in that enormous room with Pippa curled up beside me like a friendly dog, I had space to think and turn over all of the following in no particular order.

(a) Since leaving the Valley of the Thrushes my head was full of more people than ever before and I felt a responsibility to try to help them. In other words, it was beginning to dawn on me that being the president's daughter actually meant something. It wasn't about being invited to parties or getting big discounts in shoe shops or having teachers give you a higher grade than you deserved. Whether I liked it or not, people seemed to need something from me.

(b) Gangs were roaming the Badlands attacking anyone and everyone and the AOT was fighting our government, wanting to get rid of all the immigrants who had fled the fires and the floods in their own lands – and I had to stop myself from imagining what had happened to Daisy and Cordelia's father and brother and the young man Cordelia had hoped to marry. But try as I might, horrible, scary thoughts wormed their way into my head and I prayed really hard and fervently to the God who had spared our island to protect me from them. (I know this sounds a bit hypocritical, given that I'm not big on God and religion, but if God does exist, I hope He's beyond holding a grudge against teenage girls. If he does hold grudges, then what does that say about him?)

(c) Why were the AOT in the area? What were they after? Had they a purpose in mind? Was I their purpose? Or was I just going insane? But if they were here because I was here … That really freaked me out.

I tried to talk myself out of my fears. Come on, Val, I told myself, you're a fourteen-year-old girl with a flat chest on a little adventure, tucked up safe and sound in a comfy bed, surrounded by border guards. Stop thinking you're more important than you are. That worked pretty well until I remembered what Cordelia had said about the rumours that I was coming to visit, which meant that the AOT could be after me and that wasn't megalomania on my part. And if they were after me there was no telling what they might do to me or Pippa. Oh, God! Why the hell did I ever agree to this trip?

After a short period of hyperventilating (which didn't wake Pippa – a bit of a disappointment, that, because I thought my distress merited at least one person to witness it, which is twisted and wrong, I know, but it's impossible to stay lost in one single emotion without your mind running off in different irrelevant directions), my brain got back to thinking.

(d) If the AOT knew I was here, who had told them? I knew it wasn't Pippa. She was right about one thing: I did love her and I knew she loved me and I knew she would never betray me.

Then there was Joshua. Joshua reminded me of my father: it was hard to know what he was thinking. I didn't always feel comfortable around him, but did I trust him? Yes, I did. Mattie had said I should trust him and, call it intuition, or maybe I was becoming a good judge of character, but whatever it was I knew that there was no way that Joshua was a traitor.

So that left two. You-know-who and Thomas. I wanted Thomas to be my chief suspect, the one I could hate, the one who didn't mean anything to me to begin with and who wouldn't cost me a thought to condemn as the betrayer, the Judas Iscariot of my life, but my brain wouldn't go there.

So that left Damian. Was it possible he'd told the AOT I was going to be here? No, that couldn't be. Remember how Damian had asked Pippa all those questions and comforted her when she cried? That wasn't an act. That was the real Damian, the same Damian who comforted me when we were together in his room when I got sad thinking about Mattie. I trusted him more than I'd ever trusted anyone before.

Then something I hadn't thought of before came to me: had terrible things happened to him? Had the AOT tortured him when they held him captive before the ransom was paid? Was that why he had hardly spoken since we left the Valley of the Thrushes? He might be scared out of his wits … All this thinking around and around made me dizzy and I wondered if I did know the real Damian. And if I didn't, did it really matter?

I couldn't turn my mind off. No, the switch was broken. No sooner had my thoughts stopped racing about one thing than they started on another, such as, what were my mum and dad doing? Were they worried about me? If my father found out about this trip, Joshua would be carved up and fed to the dogs. Which made me laugh until I realised that that's not really funny because it's the kind of thing that actually does happen in the Badlands.

And there was other stuff too, like, was there a file on the Devereauxes? Of course there was. I wondered if Dad had read it. And were they vetted before the army took over some of their land and buildings? I knew the answer to that without having to think very hard.

I pulled the covers tighter around me. I so wanted to see Mattie but I also just wanted to wrap myself up and stay safe and warm. I must have fallen asleep in the end, because when I woke up there was sunshine in the room and I was smiling because today I was going to meet Mattie. Mattie, who wanted to help people. Mattie, who thought that we should let as many people onto our island as it could fit. Mattie, who wanted to show his solidarity with everyone in need – black, white, pink or green. Mattie, my favourite person in the world. Mattie, the son my father never mentioned.

Pippa and I ate breakfast in the big kitchen with Cordelia. We could hear Mrs Devereux clattering around the house, singing a tuneless song, but Daisy was nowhere to be seen and I didn't think it polite to ask too many questions.

If Cordelia felt any embarrassment about the night before, she didn't show it. She was busy frying eggs and bread, which didn't strike me as the kind of food I imagined an old family like hers ate in the morning. Anyway, it tasted delicious and I dismissed any scruples regarding my cholesterol, arteries and heart and tucked in (not forgetting my table manners, for Cordelia was a lady who knew and cared about these things – I could tell, believe me – even if most of the world neglected them).

It was Pippa who asked about the boys, notable by their absence, though by now I got the idea that Sandybrook House was a female place and I could work out that Joshua, Thomas and Damian were down in the barracks having breakfast with the border guards.

I liked sitting there in that big kitchen with Pippa and half-mad Cordelia, even if I was impatient to be off to meet Mattie. For some reason I couldn't figure out, I wasn't freaked when, in the middle of saying something normal, she stopped and stared. Whatever she was looking at, it wasn't any earthly thing I could see. And then she'd come out of her little trance and continue talking as if nothing had happened.

I began to get this fanciful idea that Cordelia was a latter-day visionary with prophetic power and Pippa and I had come to Sandybrook to consult her, which made sense in a nonsensical kind of way. There were her sudden moments of freezing and gazing off somewhere. And there was the fact that she seemed to know I would stay in Sandybrook before it had even been decided, so it wasn't exactly unfounded. Even so, I surprised myself when I blurted out, 'Will I meet my brother Mattie today?'

Cordelia didn't look at all surprised. In fact, she answered as if it was the most natural question in the world. 'If he is careful, no harm will come to him.'

Now, in the cold light of day, this might not seem

like much of an answer. You could pass it off as exactly the kind of thing a nice lady might say to a young girl. On the other hand, you could interpret it as something profound and prophetic, especially when you're out of your comfort zone and you want your brother, the best brother in the world, to be OK. So that's what I did.

And then, as if the spell had broken, Cordelia told us she had to see to the hens and check the one cow they still milked.

Later, when there was still no sign of Joshua, Thomas and Damian, Pippa and I wandered down towards the steward's house. It was lovely roaming around Sandybrook. The sun was high and apart from a few birds chirruping away to their hearts' content, there was nothing to disturb the silence. I felt this teeny, weeny bit of envy for the Pilgrims, because they got to play happy hippies all the time, whereas this kind of thing only happens to me once in a blue moon. (Come to think of it, I have absolutely no idea what a blue moon is, which, I suppose, is the point?)

But the hippy, dippy, trippy mood evaporated fairly rapido when we got near the steward's house, the army HQ. There was a lot of activity, and I mean a lot: soldiers whizzing here and there, looking very purposeful and serious, although I was surprised at how young they were: they all looked about sixteen. Whatever they were up to, it wasn't trying to impress me and Pippa. That was a bit disappointing, but also worrying because it meant something important was happening, and important and army and guns are not a good combination, no matter what way you look at it.

And then I realised what a great big dumb-ass idiot I was. Eureka moment. The AOT weren't after me; they were after Mattie. The AOT wanted to get rid of all the climate refugees and restore the island to the Tribe. Mattie and Solidarity wanted to help the newcomers. To the AOT Mattie was the ENEMY. They must have been following him and then realised something was up, and now they were closing in on him. While I wasn't about to appear on a TV quiz show with my chosen topic as 'The Current Political and Military Situation on Our Island', I knew that the AOT were the Bad Guys and Mattie's Solidarity were the Good Guys, even if the government (in other words, my father) did not approve of Solidarity supporting illegal immigrants. But would our soldiers help Mattie if he was in trouble? If the orders were not to, then I was bloody well going to demand that they change them. Immediately.

There were another million zillion questions buzzing around my head, but I'll only bore you with one or two, namely, why did Dad go into frozen mood when Mattie's name was mentioned? And why did he never speak about Mattie? He acted as if Mattie's name was contaminated whenever someone mentioned it. So, big deal, Mattie was helping illegal immigrants and the State of Free Citizens was big on keeping illegal immigrants out, but still, Mattie was doing it for the best of motives. Did Dad not see that?

Much as I would have liked to turn these interesting thoughts over in my head, I didn't, because I was seized by an urgent need to make Mattie safe, so I forgot to feel self-conscious and act all girly around the sentries at the door and demanded to talk to Joshua immediately regarding an issue of the greatest importance.

And that's what happened. Pippa and I waltzed right in there and a sentry knocked on a door and informed whoever was inside that the two ladies had come to see Mr Joshua.

Joshua came out and smiled when he saw us, but I could tell he was deep in the middle of something and it wasn't tiddlywinks or snakes and ladders. I didn't bother smiling back but demanded to know if Mattie was safe and if our soldiers would help him if he were ambushed or attacked by the enemy.

Joshua remained calm. He guided Pippa and me into the room which, looking back, just shows what an incredibly cool customer Joshua is. The room had a big table in the centre and giant, old-fashioned maps on the walls. At one end there was some fancy-pantsy imaging device.

The only other person in the room was an officer, about the same age as my father, who had a mild expression and who wore gold-rimmed spectacles. His uniform was the crispest I had ever seen – if they gave out medals for best-turned-out officer in the armed forces, I'd say this particular officer was a gold medal certainty. He stood when he saw me and extended his hand.

'Miss O'Connor, I presume,' he said. 'It's an honour to meet you. I'm Colonel Hugh MacDonald. Your father and I are old friends.' This, I confess, took the wind out of my sails, but I wasn't going to be diverted by a charm offensive from a smooth-talking slime-ball with a dead-fish handshake. (OK, I know I have to curb this rush to instant judgement but, in fairness, I am more often right than wrong.)

'Will the army help my brother?' I asked without bothering with the polite chit-chat and ten-minute waffle that generally goes with formal introductions.

'There are two units of frontier guards standing by across the river. They are in radio contact with your brother. He is perfectly safe. Now, may I offer you tea?'

At this, I relaxed a little. I introduced Pippa and we all sat down and had a cup of tea until the colonel excused himself and I turned to Joshua, wanting the lowdown on what was happening.

Of course I didn't get it right away, all in a rush, the way I wanted it. No, this was Joshua. So everything had to be done in a measured way. He spoke slowly, in a low voice, and he was excessively polite and considerate of my feelings to the point that I wanted to bash his head in with a plaster statue or any other object that might have served the same purpose, only there was nothing to hand which, at the time, seemed like a great pity.

Anyway, after an age, he got to the point. 'Matthew arrived in the territory last evening. Like us, he wished to pass unnoticed and only brought two soldiers with him. Unfortunately, his movements were tracked by the enemy. He suspects there may be a spy in Solidarity who planted a tracking device. He has requested me to escort you home as a meeting in the present circumstances would prove too dangerous for all concerned. Unfortunately it also makes it impossible to continue our proposed trip.'

'No way. No friggin' way. We've come this far. I'm not giving up now. If Mattie is safe, why can't I go to him?'

'Too many people know you are here. Trying to arrange a rendezvous now would put too many people's lives at risk.'

'Well, whose fault is that? Who told Colonel what's-his-name? Wasn't me.'

'I had to explain the situation to the colonel,' Joshua said, 'to secure his assistance in protecting Matthew.'

'Joshua is right, Val,' Pippa chipped in.

'Whose side are you on?'

'Yours.'

Joshua and Miss Florence Nightingale with her breasts and concerned expression were looking at me, waiting for me to concede to the inevitable logic of the situation. Oh boy, I really wanted to throw a tantrum, dance on my feet, scream, shout, and generally cause a commotion – but I didn't. Instead, I just sat there clenching and unclenching my fist and, despite a massive effort of self-control, I filled up to cry. Life can be so frustrating.

'I really wanted to see Mattie,' I said at last in a little girl's voice I hardly recognised as my own. To be fair to Joshua and Pippa, they had the decency not to answer. 'Can I at least speak to him?'

'For security reasons – for his security – we do not call him. He makes contact with us.'

I didn't bother arguing or saying that sounded stupid. I just sat there feeling completely dejected. We might have stayed there for a long time had Miss Pippa Petersen not asked a question which brought me back to the here and now.

'Where are Damian and Thomas?'

That's how I learned that Damian was in the sick bay with a bad fever and delirium. So here I was, still inside the Green Zone with no prospect of travelling further, no prospect of seeing Mattie, and Damian doing his best to expire. Sometimes life sucks.

I know what you're thinking: sick bay, army, field hospital, amputated limbs, metal beds, trauma – rough and ready. Well, that's what I was thinking. But I was wrong because the sick bay turned out to be a child's room in the old house, with pink walls, lace curtains and a wooden bed frame that was painted white. Damian was hooked up to a drip and Thomas sat by his bedside, wiping Damian's brow with a damp cloth and saying soothing words when he murmured in his sleep. And if the child's room threw me, so too did the sight of Thomas nursing Damian.

I recognised in an instant that I no longer thought about Thomas in a bad way any more. I didn't dwell on this, though, because my attention was on Damian. It was clear he'd been sedated.

I more or less pushed Thomas away and sat by

Damian's bedside and the others had the tact to leave us alone. After a while, I lay down on the bed. I know he felt my presence, because his breathing grew easier and I talked to him and recalled everything that had happened between us since we'd first met six months before. Lying beside him was the most natural thing in the world, as normal as breathing, and our breathing fell into a shared rhythm.

I knew I was heading into dangerous waters where thousands of girls had perished before. I really understand him. He's not as bad as people say. I see the real him. I can save him.

Yeah, sister, believe that if you must. But I think two paracetemol and a large dose of reality might be a better bet.

I was not blind to the irony of the situation: here I was, Little Miss Superior, who laughed at the girls in school when they swooned over obvious losers; who cracked up when she saw girls, even one or two fairly normal human beings, dissolve into shapeless butter over bad boys who treated them like shit because these deluded girls thought they were in love; and love, as we all know, turns mad criminals into harmless puppies. Yeah, right.

So it was an interesting place for me to be, playing the role of the Girl who would Save the Broken Boy. As in, Damian, my little broken boy. I want to make you better. I want to save you. I want to wrap you up in warm blankets and hold your hand and love you for ever.

Well, like I say, I wasn't blind to the ridiculousness of my situation. I knew how silly I might seem to others, not to mention myself. But there it was. I was that girl. I felt connected to Damian and I didn't envisage that connection breaking any time soon. I knew that my being there, lying beside him and speaking to him about ordinary things, the things we shared, had taken his fear away.

It wasn't just about him. Being there made my heart beat slower – not faster, as everyone says, but slower. I felt this tremendous, powerful calm descend upon me and with it a courage that I thought would allow me to face any danger whatsoever. It was a brilliant feeling but absolute rubbish, as I would soon find out.

Speaking of sleep, I slept. Not for long. It was Joshua who woke me, shaking me gently, looking down at me with those eyes of his that bored into you and which could be really freaky or, like now, very gentle and kind.

As was his custom, when things needed to get done, Joshua got straight to the point. The border guards had swept the area and it was safe for us to travel back to the Pilgrim community. He had consulted with Colonel MacDonald, who advised that we leave immediately. The colonel had offered us a different vehicle, a four-wheel drive with the markings of an ambulance – an old trick, Joshua said, but a good one. The colonel also offered a military escort but Joshua believed this would draw attention to us, so he declined. Joshua said we'd take a more direct route back, away from the border region, so there should be no danger.

The ambulance was more than cosmetic, because Damian was still weak and drowsy under the influence of the medicine they had given him, so we really had a patient to transport home. It was ironic and a little cruel to think that Damian, who was all gung-ho for adventure and going off to do what a man has to do, was the one who had turned flaky.

He was so wobbly that we used a wheelchair to bring him to the ambulance. I'm sure we made a quaint picture – the two pale girls, the pale boy in the wheelchair, the Ethiopian prince, the young Masai warrior – just the sort of group you see every day in the Green Zone in the old County of Kilkenny, or whatever this place used to be called before the State of Free Citizens was established.

Passing the sentries on the door, I noticed the difference in them. They stood to attention and saluted as we passed and I caught the eye of one as he tried to get a look at me. No doubt Colonel MacDonald had told them who the visitors were.

I knew that Mum would have known exactly how to behave in my position and so I did my best to act the way I thought she would have. I smiled to acknowledge the salute, but not in a way that might suggest I was laughing at them or turning up my nose or pretending to be superior. I tried to be polite, grateful and dignified. I'd hate to see a photograph of that smile, if one existed.

And though I didn't say this out loud to myself, I suppose I was becoming more and more open to a possibility that I'd never considered much before this visit, which was that the daughter of the president meant something to the people on the island and I'd better remember that and try to act accordingly. And next time there was a state reception and I had my photograph taken with my father and my mother, I wouldn't act like it was some great inconvenience or say 'Who'd want to see a photograph of me?'

Damian was placed on a stretcher bed which ran crossways in the rear compartment of the jeep, so he had to bend up his knees to fit. There was a single seat near where his head lay, and I sat there, ready to nurse him if he needed it. Pippa sat in the middle of the jeep and Thomas sat with Joshua up front. The windows were darkened, which added a bit of mystery to the whole escapade. The colonel, whose uniform looked even more impressive in the sunlight, if such a thing were possible, came out and waved us off.

It was thirty hours since we'd left the Valley of the Thrushes. It seemed like a lifetime. I was glad to be going home. I felt tired. I wanted my own room in my own house, even if it was cleaned a zillion times a day. I wanted some space to figure out what I knew now that I didn't know before.

It was crap that I hadn't met Mattie, but I sensed his presence and that, in its own way, was reassuring. I was wearing his old sweater and that made me feel close to him. It was disappointing (but also a relief, truth be told) that we had not, after all, crossed into the Amber Zone or further to the Great River and the Badlands that lay beyond it – I reckoned I had more than enough to be going on with. Cordelia and her family had opened a door for me and I'd glimpsed what was on the other side.

We travelled in silence. Because I was in the back I could see everyone in the jeep. We felt like a family. No, I hadn't gone soft in the head. I was serious. You know some people for years but never get to know them. You spend a few hours with others and you know them. There's a bond you form and nothing will break it. That's how I felt then about our group.

Yeah, Thomas might irritate me by trying to be too helpful, but I understood him now and liked him. So you have to scrub that stuff I said about him only being interested in himself. I saw the way he sat beside Damian; I saw the way he idolised Joshua. What I had taken to be selfishness was just naivety.

And Joshua? Well, Joshua was a long-lost soulmate of my father. I'm sure they were related way back when.

I was content for him to lead us and show us the way home.

Pippa and Damian were just Pippa and Damian, my best friends, the two people I loved most in the world. So it was soothing and comforting to sit there locked in our little jeep, cruising through the countryside on our way home, thinking my thoughts.

Home. There were things I wanted to talk with Dad about. Serious things. About the Army of the Tribe and Solidarity and the situation beyond the safety of the Green Zone. I wanted to help, too, in whatever way I could, not in a big song and dance way, not in a Joan-of-Arc, save-the-world way, but in a real way, if such a thing were possible.

One thing I'd learned was that the situation outside the Citadel and the Green Zone was far less stable and peaceful than I'd realised. And if it was as bad in the Amber Zone as Cordelia's story suggested, what must it be like in the Badlands?

And Pippa's family? What way were their lives? She was worried, really worried. I could see that. Even an idiot could figure out that things were ropey on the island and Pippa was not an idiot. Nothing, and I mean nothing, was lost on her. Her brain absorbed every last drop of information. If I felt the unease in the air, then she felt it ten times more keenly.

As I was thinking this, Pippa turned and looked at me and smiled one of her shy smiles. That girl! I swear she could read my mind. In someone else it would have been scary.

Then Joshua got in on the telepathic lark.

'Everything all right, Miss Valentina?'

'Yes, thank you, Joshua. Everything's fine.'

For a moment I thought it was me who had caused what happened next.

It took me a few seconds to begin to understand what was happening. There was a sudden jolt and I was thrown forward and crashed into Damian, which, in fairness, did not do him a whole lot of good.

And then something was raining down on my head and I put my hands over it to protect myself. Almost immediately we lurched forward, only to come to an abrupt halt. The rain turned out to be dust and flecks of glass from the shattered windows of the jeep. I pushed open the back door and staggered out. A massive tree lay across the road. The heavy branches had smashed the glass, though this was something I only figured out a long time after the event, when I managed to speak to Pippa and compare notes. But immediately, right there, I was too dazed to put all the pieces of the jigsaw together. My brain wasn't working on full power or anything like it.

I remember standing behind the jeep, rubbing my head and running my hand inside the neck of my sweater to shake loose the bits of glass that were stuck to me. I touched my nose and felt blood oozing from a cut. That freaked me out a little bit, especially when I found a few more nicks and cuts and all of them were bleeding.

This may sound like it took forever, but it was only a few seconds. After that everything is very hazy. I do have snatches of memory, like vivid images from an old film: Pippa at my side saying, 'I think Joshua is badly hurt'; me seeing Joshua slumped over the steering wheel, a big gash on his head and a frightening amount of dark ruby blood flowing from it; Thomas trying to pull me away from the jeep, telling me to hide, shouting and crying at the same time.

Then there was a helicopter and soldiers running up – our soldiers coming to rescue us. I was so relieved. I distinctly remember my feeling of relief.

Thomas ran to the first soldier. He was shouting that Joshua was injured and needed help. I'll never forget, never, ever, ever forget the sound when the soldier swung his rifle and smashed Thomas on the head. I swear I heard his skull crack.

Before I could scream or protest or faint or react in any way, I was tackled to the ground by another soldier.

I wish I could say I fought like a tiger and scratched his eyes out but I didn't. He punched me really hard in the stomach and I was too sore and stunned to put up any resistance.

Two of them dragged me to the helicopter and threw me in. My hands were tied behind my back and I was made to lie face down. There was more commotion in the helicopter. I heard Damian shouting 'no'. I tried to lift my head to see what was happening but someone pushed me down hard and put his boot on my neck. I heard Damian's voice again, calling out my name, and then there was gunfire and the helicopter lifted from the ground and I couldn't hear Damian any more.

'Oh, God,' I prayed, 'please don't let anything happen to Damian, please.'

I tried to stay calm but I was beginning to hyperventilate. This is a rescue mission, I told myself. These are our soldiers. It's OK. Everything is going to be fine. That's the kind of crap you tell yourself when things are hopeless, when you're lying tied and there's a soldier standing on your head. This isn't as bad as it seems. This is really quite a good situation. Right. It makes sense in a way: I mean, when all hope is gone, what can you do? Trust in miracles, that's what.

I was doing pretty well on the miracle-believing front when my stomach began to do somersaults. I felt as queasy and nauseous as I had in the jeep when we'd left the Valley of the Thrushes. But here's the thing:

did you ever try to throw up when your face is pushed into the floor?

I needed to sit up. I really began to panic, as in big-time panic. I started to thrash about like a fish in the bottom of a boat, thrash for all I was worth until a voice, a voice that made me afraid, really afraid, called out, 'What the f*** is going on?' and when I heard that voice any tiny, weeny little bit of hope that this was a rescue mission was snuffed out, never to be reignited. At that moment, all I wanted to do was die.

I might have died if the soldier standing on my head had not been pushed off and I was yanked upright, whereupon I threw up all over Pippa. If that upset her, she did a damned good job of hiding it, because she simply hugged me tight and held on to me. And, possibly because of the unsavoury nature of what I had spewed out, our captors let us be. For a few minutes, my breathing was haywire, what with the panic and the awful feeling of suffocation I'd experienced before Pippa saved me. But bit by bit it came back to normal.

I kept my eyes shut really tight. That made our situation somehow more bearable, not seeing anything, not looking at anyone. It was so comforting, so unbelievably comforting to have Pippa with me. And even as I wondered why they had taken her too I knew the answer: in the few seconds it took to snatch us, they weren't sure which one of us was which. Think about it: we were both wearing the same kind of clothes; we were both pale and white-skinned; we both had blue eyes and light-coloured hair and, leaving aside the translucent stuff and her curves, we were really pretty alike. Like sisters. Sure, they'd have seen photographs of me in the papers, but we were snatched in an instant and they didn't hang around to examine us closely and decide who was who. They probably knew by now but that didn't matter. Pippa was here.

I hung onto her with fierce determination. Breathing evenly again, I told myself that I had at least three reasons to be grateful: (1) We were alive, (2) we were together, (3) we were like sisters. That was the credit side.

But then, once the word 'credit' came into my mind, it was immediately followed by its opposite.

Debit.

And when I began to reckon the debit side of the equation – Joshua injured; Thomas with a smashed skull; Damian possibly dead; Pippa and me captured – I thought it safer to concentrate on the good things, being alive and being together, and forget about everything else, though you can imagine how successful that turned out to be as a strategy.

I don't know how long we flew; I don't know how high or how fast or in what precise direction. What I do know is that after what was probably a short time, though it seemed like eternity to the two of us, the helicopter landed and I opened my eyes. Though I didn't know it at the time, we had flown across the Amber Zone and the Great River and were now in the Badlands.

I opened my eyes.

There were two guards in the helicopter and two in the cockpit.

'Where are we?' I asked.

The guard who'd stood on my head leered at me and answered, 'Where your father doesn't rule.'

'The Badlands?'

'Our land,' he said.

I knew then that we had been taken by the AOT. The guard was really horrible. But I didn't have to look at him for long, because both Pippa and I were blindfolded then. In the helicopter, I couldn't bear to open my eyes even though I was free to do so. Now I wanted to look around to find out at last what the Badlands looked like and I wasn't allowed to. That sucked. But clearly I was recovering my spirit because things only suck when you have a bit of fight in you so that, at least, was a sign of life.

We were brought from the chopper and put into yet another jeep (how many jeeps are there on this benighted island?). Pippa and I were put on the seat behind the driver. I knew from the voices that there were two soldiers in the front and one in the seat behind. (I say 'soldiers' because the ones in the helicopter were dressed like our soldiers, but we had no way of knowing if the others in the jeep were dressed the same. In my mind's eye they were soldiers, though they could have been wearing Italian suits and silk shirts for all I know.)

And then another one sat in beside me on the seat. 'Push over,' he said. It was the leery one from the helicopter, the one who stood on my head. He certainly wasn't the sharpest knife in the drawer and, in normal circumstances, he would have been no match for my rapier-like wit but, sitting here beside me, deliberately putting his weight against me, was a whole different bunch of bananas. Anyone who has experienced the thrill and excitement of another human body pushing against you in a tight space, when that body belongs to a person about whom you dream at night, knows that's a pretty cool experience, like the time Damian and I were thrown together on the tram heading towards the Valley of the Thrushes. But this was the opposite of that kind of feeling. Gorilla Boy leaning into me and breathing his sour, garlicky breath over me was sickening and intimidating. And then he put his hand on my leg and started rubbing it up and down and I reacted so violently he laughed out loud. But it wasn't an amused laugh. It was a laugh that said, So you think I'm disgusting, do you? Well, I'm going to get you, you little bitch, and then we'll see what disgusting is.

'You leave her alone,' Pippa said, and the other soldiers laughed and began to mock Gorilla Boy and he moved away a bit, but I knew we hadn't heard the last of him.

I'm not saying I got used to being blindfolded but on that short journey I absorbed and interpreted every sound I could hear. In fact I felt one hundred per cent alive and intended to stay that way for as long as I could. That was the survival instinct kicking in. I was listening to the voices, trying to decide who might become an ally if we needed one.

There was one voice in the jeep, the guard sitting behind us, who sounded like a good human being. There was no malice in his voice and you could imagine him having a sister or maybe two. Even in wars, soldiers remember their families. Keep that in mind, I told myself.

It didn't take me long to get the hang of things in the world beyond the Green Zone and the outer frontier. It was war. A week ago I had been living in my own little bubble and even if I got back home, there was no way I could pretend that all was well on the island. It wasn't. I was in the Badlands, in a world where the old rules didn't apply and I'd better learn the new ones pretty quickly.

We didn't have far to travel, twenty minutes maybe, and then we stopped and were pushed out of the jeep and my hands were untied. There was a hum in the air and sounds of activity and machinery. We were directed away from the jeep and told to lie down on our bellies. I held Pippa's hand and squeezed it tight.

'Are you going to shoot us?' I asked, my voice sounding steadier and calmer than I was.

'No.' It was the kind soldier. 'I'm going to remove your blindfolds. Don't move; don't look up; don't speak.'

I felt him bend down towards me and untie the knot. I was lying on the bare earth. I turned to Pippa and we smiled encouragement at each other. 'Use the ladder and climb down,' the soldier said. I raised my head enough to see him. He was young, in his twenties, tall and broad. He was wearing grey combats and a grey T-shirt and hoodie. He was handsome in an athletic kind of way. On his shoulder he had a gun.

'Quickly.'

'Where?'

'Behind you.'

I looked over my shoulder. There was a pit of some kind with a ladder sticking up over the top.

'Move,' he said, and I knew we had exhausted his store of goodwill and fraternity for the moment, so we moved, first Pippa and then me.

The pit turned out to be a rough shelter, lined with timber, about eight feet deep and six feet square. There were two blankets, a saucepan of water, a bowl of apples and an empty bucket. That was it. Even as we were looking around and wondering, our friend started to pull up the ladder. It was halfway up before we realised what was happening and what it meant.

'No!' I shouted. 'You can't leave us down here!'

But he could. And he did. And then it got worse because as we stood looking up, protesting and shouting up at him, the nice boy with two imaginary sisters pulled a cover across the pit and, bit by bit, the light disappeared until we were left in total darkness.

Total darkness.

Plus, we both smelt of vomit. Stale vomit.

Are you claustrophobic? Are you afraid of the dark? Did you ever imagine being buried alive? Do you think about the worms and the way they'll eat your body? Yes? So you can imagine our predicament. We were stuck in a hole in the ground that was basically a large-ish coffin. Was I scared? Was I terrified? Was I hysterical? In a word, yes. Pippa and I found each other and sat down and wrapped ourselves in the blankets. It seemed safer that way, wrapped up in our woollen shrouds. We were in a strange and truly horrible place. This was let's-go-out-of-our-minds territory.

How airtight was our bunker? Not too much, we prayed. Because it was dark and freaky, not to mention freezing cold and stony, we spoke in whispers. And any time there was the merest touch of something I jumped out of my skin. Pippa was pretty freaked out too, but she did manage to find the saucepan of water and cupped some into her hand and said it tasted fine, so we knew we wouldn't die of thirst. That was a comfort.

Then she found the apples and we knew we wouldn't die of starvation either. We ate one each, but an apple after you've puked your guts up is not easy on the stomach.

There was a bucket. Well, you can guess what that was for. I didn't have to use it too much during our time in the hole but I'm not superwoman – I had to use it for peeing, but no way was I going to evacuate my bowels in the presence of another person in a six foot wide hole. No way. And although we didn't discuss it, Pippa must have decided the same thing and that suited me just fine. The smell of vomit and urine were quite enough unpleasantness in the olfactory department.

I reckoned it was about 3 p.m. when we entered the pit and we stayed there until the next morning, which means that we spent about sixteen hours there before anyone came near us. Sixteen hours in the dark in a hole in the ground.

So what did we do down there for that length of time? We imagined the worst. We cried. We felt sick.

We whispered. We compared notes. We tried to figure out what was happening. We tried to keep ourselves going. We tried to be brave.

Watching old detective series' on TV paid off, because we were pretty good at figuring things out. Like, the kidnap must have been opportunistic because it didn't seem as if they were ready for us. Or that Colonel MacDonald had to be the one who tipped them off. I didn't like him from the moment I set eyes on him – too smooth by half, with his immaculate uniform and manners. 'I'm an old friend of your father's.' Some frigging friend. Manners mean nothing. They're only for show. They tell you nothing about the person behind them. I knew that now. (Sorry, Damian.)

We had already figured our captors were the AOT because they were the Bad Guys. They must have been so pleased to have captured the president's daughter. We were probably being held for a ransom, in the same way Damian and his mother had been held. Of course, I regretted not asking him more questions about his experience. But it was reassuring that he was released and we hoped we would be too.

When we got tired of playing Sherlock Holmes and Watson, tired of worrying ourselves sick about the worst thing that could happen and exhausted from imagining the rats and other unspeakables grubbing in the earth on all sides of us, Pippa told me her favourite fairytale, The Snow Queen. I pictured myself as Gerda and Damian was Kay, and we lived in a cosy cottage in the forest with a roaring fire and a thousand candles and, on the stove, there was a steaming pot of vegetable soup. A week ago I was turning my nose up at vegetable soup in the Valley of the Thrushes and now I was salivating at the thought of a bowl. That's what war does to people – it makes them re-evaluate.

When Pippa finished her story, I told her the story of 'The Steadfast Tin Soldier', which was probably not the wisest choice, seeing as how both the soldier and his lovely ballerina end up perishing in fire. But on the other hand, I'm not sure there is an appropriate tale for two young girls held captive in a pit by the AOT. We both knew that everything we did was a tactic designed to divert our minds from thinking about where we were and what might happen to us when we were let out.

Then we played another diversionary game. What kind of animals are we, trapped in a pit? Tigers, with pent-up energy, who would tear our captors to shreds. Snakes, who would uncoil themselves and shoot poison into our enemies' veins. You get the idea. We were keeping ourselves psychologically strong. At one point, I said we were like Pooh Bear the time he went hunting for heffalumps and that set me off giggling till my psychological strength ebbed away.

Some time before morning I fell into a fitful sleep from which I awoke stiff and sore and cold in my bones and in my heart. I felt old. My legs ached and I remembered the nights when I was seven or eight and my mother rubbed my legs and told me not to worry, that the soreness was growing pains and it meant I was becoming a beautiful young woman. Well, I felt neither young nor beautiful, but the pains were back. How I wished that my mother could be with me now to reassure me and soothe away my aches and pains. Oh, God! It was all so awful.

I sensed it must be morning but there was no way of telling. Somewhere along the way I'd lost my watch. And sitting there in the dark, hungry, greedy for light, I thought about the other things I'd lost, including my rucksack with my diary. I blushed in the darkness remembering the things I'd written about Damian; sappy, sentimental things that should never see the light of day. And other things too, not sentimental or mushy, but private: my thoughts on Joshua and Thomas, not to mention my mother and father. I pictured some member of the AOT laughing his head off at my private thoughts.

And then I heard the world waking up. Not loud and clear; faintly, dimly – but I heard it. And I felt like Pippa's Moonshine, all alert and listening, wanting to bark, wanting to make someone take notice of me but afraid for fear of attracting the attention of the wrong people.

There was a scratching sound and the cover was opened a little and then it was pulled right off and the sun flooded in and I had to close my eyes because the light was too bright, too sudden, too painful after the prolonged blackness.

This sudden uncovering made me feel exposed, almost naked, and defenceless like a newborn baby. Also, I was afraid that the person who pulled back the cover might be the one from the chopper, Gorilla Boy, and I didn't fancy the prospect of him leering down on me. But it wasn't him. It was a girl and she wasn't hostile or aggressive, though she wasn't friendly either. She was just businesslike.

She told me to tie the bucket to a rope she lowered and advised me to stand back in case the contents spilled out. She didn't have to ask me twice. The bucket was passed up and when it came back it smelt of disinfectant.

By this stage Pippa was awake too. She had this brilliant knack of going from sleep to wakefulness in one movement with none of the moaning, groaning, eyes half-open intermediate stages that most people pass through. No. With Pippa she was either fast asleep or fully awake. And it was she who asked the girl if we could have some food for breakfast and the girl said she'd see what she could do.

'Thank you,' I said, looking up and shielding my eyes so I could see her face.

'You're welcome,' she answered in a polite, distant kind of way.

She was pretty, about twenty, I reckoned, with dyed blonde hair and dark eyes. She spoke English with a heavy accent from somewhere in eastern Europe. Maybe she was a captive too, a different kind of captive, one who had to work or look after the soldiers? It was possible. Anything was possible.

She told us she would leave the roof uncovered for a short time to freshen up the air in our hiding place. Hiding place. She made it sound like we were playing a game of hide-and-seek.

With the cover off, we could hear the noise of farm machinery and motor vehicles as well as voices. A man's voice called out, 'Tanya', and the girl answered him. She was feeding hens that clucked around our grave. There may also have been a goose – there was a racket that Pippa identified as a goose but which, to tell the truth, could have been a mad dog for all I knew.

The man came near and he and Tanya spoke. We were all ears, in our hole in the earth, eavesdropping as best we could on the goings-on in the world above the ground.

His voice sounded Irish. She called him Peter. He was one of the Tribe, of course, as were all the members of the AOT. They didn't say much of interest at first, but you could tell they were more than just friends or acquaintances. I wondered did people think the same about me and Damian when they heard us talk together? Was it always so obvious when two people were attracted to each other?

My mind swam in thoughts of you-know-who, and from Damian my thoughts spiralled out of control and I sank down against the wall of our bunker and curled up and cried. It was pretty simple: I was here and I wanted to be home. I wanted to be in my own room, to stroke Eccles and speak with my mum and my dad. I missed them and I missed Geraldine and Francesca and Pilgrim John and silly Gwen. I even missed ridiculous Ms Rumsfeld and Mouldy Old Bowels, everyone and everything that passed for my life before this catastrophe began.

And then there was the gnawing worry about Damian and Joshua and Thomas, poor Thomas with his smashed head, not forgetting the little boy and his family and Cordelia and hers, so, all in all, I felt like my life had collapsed and caved in and was fast filling up with clay, which was a pretty apt metaphor given that I was sitting in a hole in the earth with no knowledge of what was in store for us.

On top of all that my tummy was rumbling and grumbling and reminding me that, apart from an apple and a little water, it hadn't been fed for twenty-four hours, and that particular meal of fried bread and eggs had been ejected in mid-air all over Pippa, whose sweatshirt smelt sour, like fermented fruit. I was aware that I hadn't had a wash for a while either, or cleaned my teeth, brushed my hair or changed my underwear, and I felt that my period was coming. So, in short, I wasn't in a good place. Pippa snuggled up beside me and we wrapped our arms around each other and hung on for dear life.

And that's how we were when Gorilla Boy, the one who'd stood on my neck, crushed against me in the jeep and grabbed my leg, showed up and looked down on us.

'Two little lesbians,' he sneered.

He didn't have to say another word – in those three he'd shown himself for the homophobic, misogynist creep that he was. I don't think the AOT was a good place for gay guys or girls. Mind you, the State of Free Citizens was not exactly the most liberal place on the planet when it came to matters of sexual orientation, but that's a story for another day.

Gorilla Boy enjoyed his moment of power, looking down on us with this leery, lecherous, pervy expression on his face. 'Want me to come down and join the loving?' he said.

I recovered myself sufficiently to do my best mother impersonation.

'What's happening now?' I asked.

'You're being moved.'

'Where to?'

'You're going to see the general.'

'Thank you.'

'You're welcome, your Royal Highness. And is there anything else you'd like?'

I should have quit while I was ahead. I should have zipped it. But no, good old Val had to throw in one more little thing.

'Breakfast would be good.'

'Breakfast? I'll see what I can find.'

It wasn't long before he was back with a friend to join in the girl-baiting.

'I got something for you,' he said in a voice that sounded horrible and full of malice. And with that he tossed something down into the hole.

It was a live rat. I'll repeat that piece of information. It was a rat. A big fat rat. A big fat live rat.

Did I scream? Did I close my eyes, dance on my toes, shake my head? You may be sure I did. And then some more. And cool-as-a-cucumber Pippa, who had a Doctor Dolittle relationship with animals, wasn't far behind me. And if we were terrified, imagine how the rat felt. He was scurrying here and there and trying to run up the walls. It was pandemonium in the pit and Gorilla Boy and his pal thought it was the best sport they had had in years.

I don't know how long the episode lasted – not very long in reality – but it was too long by half. It ended with a loud crack from a rifle that blew the rat into little pieces. That was Gorilla Boy's idea of a joke. He could have killed us. It was hyperventilation time and I would have slid to the ground only I couldn't bear the idea of touching any of the little pieces of dead rat that littered the floor.

'Lower the ladder,' said a new voice, a kind voice, the voice of the soldier with the imaginary sisters, and he ordered the two hyenas to go away and laugh somewhere else. And when we had gathered what was left of our wits, he helped us out of the pit.

We were moved into the back of a truck with a canvas roof and an open back. We were made sit as far into the truck as we could. Gorilla Boy and his idiot friend were our guards. We were blindfolded. I'm not talking about the velvet blindfolds you get on an aeroplane either; let's just say that they weren't exactly soft and gentle against our skin. They wrapped this sticky tape round and round our heads. It was horrible. The tape stuck to my skin and my hair and made me feel all sweaty and just yuck, really yuck.

Pippa and I didn't say much to each other because we didn't want Gorilla Boy listening and we certainly didn't hold hands because that would have set him off again about us being you-know-what. So we sat there like mummies in the truck, being bounced around on the wooden seat.

It's funny – not funny ha-ha; funny peculiar – but not being able to see unbalances your entire body. I felt every bump in the road, every pothole, every bit of gravel. Ugh, aagh, ouch. And when the truck swung round a corner, it was like being on a rollercoaster. It was like some kind of sensory overload, as if my body was compensating for not being able to see what was happening by feeling everything more intensely by a multiple of ten – and it wasn't exciting or pleasurable or good in any way. (On the other hand, we were no longer in a hole in the ground and compared to that, being bumped around was child's play.)

Thankfully the journey didn't last too long. But it did last long enough for Gorilla Boy to start being, well, Gorilla Boy. He touched my cheek and when I shouted out, he laughed his pathetic little laugh, which reminded me just how much of a perv he was. Then he clapped his hands really loudly in front of my face. I threw my head back in fright and smacked it off one of the metal supports at the side of the truck.

Pippa must have heard the crack because she reached out immediately to me to see if I was all right and gave Gorilla Boy a piece of her mind, which was just the response he wanted and made him laugh in an ugly way.

'That's enough, now,' I said, in the same way I would have spoken to a really annoying little brother. Only he wasn't my brother; he was a gorilla and he had a gun, and we were his prisoners and we were blindfolded.

He did stop for half a minute but then he started flicking his finger against my leg hard enough for it to hurt. I wanted to kick him really hard where it would hurt, and I fantasised about seizing his gun and shooting him dead. I didn't have even one little mental reservation, which makes me sound a monster, I know, but so many strange and unreal things had happened to me in those few days that strange was the new normal.

But I didn't seize his gun or shoot him and, given what happened next, I half regret that I didn't.

I can't tell you exactly what happened, because we couldn't see, so here's what I think happened: the truck stopped. The driver didn't turn off the ignition and I could feel the vibration of the engine. There was talking and raised voices, lots of them, though they weren't angry, just excited and nervous and everyone talking together. The voices were speaking a language I didn't understand; it sounded African, but I wouldn't swear to it, as African languages hadn't featured highly in my education up to that point, so all I can say is that the voices reminded me of how Thomas spoke.

We heard and felt a surge of people and the truck shook. It wasn't a violent rocking. It was like when the wind catches a car and there's a momentary wobble, so I had no sense of threat or danger. From the wobbling,

I mean; obviously, I wasn't exactly sanguine about our situation in the broader scheme of things. Anyway, the voices were mainly women's and children's, so it wasn't as if all-out war was about to break out, which is why the sudden gunfire and the screaming that followed it were all the more shocking.

Gorilla Boy and Idiot Boy started to holler and shout, the way people do on amusement rides, and the sounds of their guns sent a shudder through my body and Pippa's too, I guessed. When you are close to someone firing a gun, an automatic machine gun, the noise is unbelievable.

I heard everything in slow motion, if you know what I mean, every scream and cry of agony of pity and despair. I heard them, all the women and children that they were shooting. I pulled and tore at the tape and ripped it off my face and Pippa did the same and we saw them standing at the back of the truck shooting. They were laughing as if it was a game or like a pair of wild dogs chasing a rabbit, just for the raw pleasure of tearing it to pieces. It was sadistic and it was sick, sick, sick.

'Stop! Stop!' we screamed, and Pippa tried to wrestle the gun out of Gorilla Boy's hands.

They did stop, though not because of us, but because the person in charge came and told them to, and his voice was so cold and hard it terrified me. It was the voice from the helicopter and he was clearly in charge.

I didn't know it then but this was Rocco, the general's right-hand man.

He looked at us. He didn't have to say another word. Pippa and I sat down and you've never seen two more silent people in your entire life. Rocco said something to the other two and then went out of sight. I couldn't see much from where I was sitting – Gorilla Boy and the other soldier blocked out most of the view – but I did see the body of a woman lying face down with blood oozing from under her bright clothes, and in the silence I heard soft moaning, though whether it was coming from inside my head or outside the truck, I couldn't tell.

Next thing, Rocco was back and he threw a bag into the truck. It clattered on the floor. I wasn't sure then what was real and what was hallucinatory.

I looked at the bag. It was green and non-descript, with a drawstring at the top. I kept looking and in my mind's eye I saw a dark place filled with gold coins, jewellery and shiny stones. Three words kept swirling round my mind: kill, plunder, trade.

Kill, plunder, trade. That's what criminals did and now the AOT had done it too. It was one thing to be opposed to immigrants, but to shoot defencelesswomen and children? So this was what life was like in the Badlands. I'd wanted to see it first-hand and now I had.

I felt completely empty. I could hardly bear to look at the two young men who had blood on their hands or to be confined in the same space as them. After the bloodletting, I think they might have felt something like shame because they sat down too, quiet and deflated. They stared out the back of the truck, not looking at me or Pippa. Maybe they wanted to be back home with their families as much as Pippa and I did. The thought kept going around my head – if they were capable of killing these women and children, they were capable of killing us too. And in total silence we finished the rest of our journey and came to the house where the general was.

The wheels on the bus go round and round, round and round, round and round, the wheels of the bus go round and round, all over town.

Well, you have to be doing something to amuse yourself or you could go mad, nuts, bonkers, start raving and acting totally deranged and doing random things like poking holes in the cuffs of your sweater and chewing the frayed bits. I was not in a good place. The whole nightmare was catching up with me.

They'd brought us to another house – an old army barracks or something similar. It was beginning to fall down. The paint was flaking off the doors and windows; there was damp mould growing on the walls and ceilings; many of the windows were broken; wooden floors sagged and the plaster on the walls was crumbling to dust.

They put us in a room on the first floor, a great big empty room that was chilly and draughty. There were two beds which were pretty serviceable and some blankets and … nothing else. And I mean nothing. Zilch. Niente. Nada.

Off the bedroom there was a bathroom with a toilet (good) and a sink which was home to assorted insects and their families (bad). When we turned the tap, the water came out (good). Unfortunately, it was a disgusting brown colour and seemed to be teeming with all kinds of animal life (bad, very bad). We let it run and it spluttered and stopped and started, and the pipes moaned and groaned, but finally water flowed from the tap and looked like water should look.

We washed as best we could. We had no soap and no towels and no hot water and no toothbrushes and no shampoo and no deodorant and no clean underwear and no sanitary towels. We had our hands and we had cold water and a sink that was discoloured and grimy in a bathroom where the window had more than its fair share of dead flies caught in spiders' webs. Charming.

We washed ourselves in stages and patted ourselves dry before washing the next little bit. It wasn't brilliant, but it was better than a hole in the ground and a bucket in the corner. (And to think I used to complain about Francesca cleaning my room and invading my privacy. Let's just say, I was growing up fast.)

We were locked in. But not for long. Rocco came and brought us down to meet the general. The barracks was fairly quiet. We didn't see Gorilla Boy or his friend, but there were two other young guys with guns, dressed in soldiers' uniforms, in the hallway, and we heard voices from somewhere deep in the building.

The general, whose name turned out to be Tadhg, was waiting for us in what must have served as his office. He was sitting behind a desk. He was small and neat and pretty handsome too, with dark eyes and a thin face. He spoke in a polite, professory kind of way. He was the sort of fellow you could imagine at home baking bread or growing marigolds or helping out with the Pilgrims at the weekends. Not in a million years would you have taken him for the leader of an army, if that's what the AOT were. General Tadhg looked pretty harmless, all the more so because he didn't bother with a uniform or any military trappings.

If you met my father, it occurred to me, and didn't know who he was, would you think he was president of the most secure state in the world? Would you think him capable of running a state where no dissent was allowed? I was not comfortable thinking about my father like that because he's my dad, but he's also President Amos O'Connor and people fear him. I know that.

Anyway, all these were the thoughts of a moment. There were two chairs on one side of the desk. Tadhg told us to sit down. A soldier brought in a tray with mugs, a teapot, milk, sugar and biscuits. It was so cosy. At any moment I was expecting Mr Tumnus and Lucy (you remember, from the Narnia books?) to pop in and join us. My goodness, it made us almost forget that we were prisoners.

How stupid did they think we were? I remembered Colonel MacWhatever and his smiles and good manners and his false face and I wasn't falling for that shit.

The general poured three cups of tea. Clearly Rocco was not invited to the tea-party. He stood apart, his back to the door, just in case we entertained thoughts of running away, I suppose. Then Tadhg offered to pour milk – no thanks, no thanks – and add the sugar – no thanks, no thanks. He handed each of us a mug.

Now, I'm as big a fan of Mahatma Gandhi as the next person – power to the people; passive resistance; we shall overcome; you may deny my body freedom, but you cannot lock up my mind, etc, etc. But I really, really wanted a nice cup of tea and a biscuit or two or ten. In fact, a ham sandwich would have been great. So I supped with the devil. I drank my tea and accepted a biscuit when he offered me one.

Pippa followed my example in everything I did, bowing to my apparently superior knowledge of diplomatic protocol. I suppose in a way that's what the encounter with General Tadhg resembled – a reception hosted by one government for the representatives of another. Though that was a dangerous kind of comparison to make. General Tadhg a representative of a government? What government? The government of the Badlands? A government whose soldiers shoot women and children for sport and rob them of their meagre possessions? Steady on, girl, I told myself.

I suddenly felt tired and not up to all this figuring out and second-guessing and trying to be adult and responsible.

'I'm pleased to meet you, Miss O'Connor,' Tadhg was saying, speaking in a very polite and civil tone.

I didn't answer.

He waited.

I studied the fire-grate.

'Give me fifteen minutes alone with her blondie friend and we'll soon see how determined Miss O'Connor is to remain silent,' Rocco said, and I didn't want to imagine what he had in mind.

Pippa said nothing but I knew she must be terrified. I was terrified too, but the thing was not to let it show.

'Why are you holding us?' I asked as calmly as I could.

'Now that she's found her tongue, can I have the other one, general?' Rocco asked casually, and I don't think I've ever heard a voice, before or since, so full of menace and cruelty.

'All in good time, Rocco,' Tadhg answered, 'all in

good time.'

'Pippa is my adopted sister,' I told him. 'My father would not want anything to happen to either of us.'

I thought that was a pretty good line, under the circumstances, and it seemed to do the trick, because Tadhg gave us an assurance of sorts.

'Nothing will happen if you do exactly as you are told. Understand?'

'Yes.'

OK, it wasn't much, but it was something. Something to hang onto.

The meeting proceeded quickly then. If we wanted to be released, I had to phone my father and tell him the ransom demand: the release of named AOT prisoners from the Hrad, the provision of specified guns and military equipment and the payment of a substantial amount of cash. The government of the State of Free Citizens would have twenty-four hours to meet the demands. If they refused, Pippa and I would be killed. The list of prisoners and military equipment was being prepared. When it was ready, I was to make the call.

Tadhg was quiet and matter-of-fact through all this, pouring more tea and passing round the biscuits, and I was my parents' daughter and responded in kind: I kept my cool, even though we were talking about my possible execution, not to mention the fact that I had to break the news to my dad myself. That was a phone call I was not exactly looking forward to making.

Pippa withdrew into herself, making herself small and almost invisible, doing that flatlining thing where she put herself into virtual suspended animation.

I was concentrating hard, keeping as outwardly calm as I could, developing an increasing admiration for the way my mum and dad conducted themselves and feeling increasingly sick inside.

When the meeting concluded, Tadhg stood and thanked me, telling me we'd meet again within the hour. Rocco showed us back to our room.

As you can imagine, I wasn't in the mood for small talk. All I wanted to do was to shut the door, lie on the bed, cry my eyes out and then start thinking how the hell we were going to get out of this mess.

Only Rocco gave no indication that he was going to leave. He followed us into the room and just stood there, a little back from the beds, loitering, watching us, and I could feel he was looking for an excuse to do something to us, harm us in some way. It was horrible, being watched like that.

Pippa and I sat together on one of the beds and instinctively we drew close and hugged each other. I tried to ignore Rocco completely, forget about him being there, make him disappear by force of will and higher mental powers, which, unsurprisingly, did not work. Even when he started talking, low at first, low but insistent, I did my best not to listen, to think happy thoughts, to sing 'My Favourite Things' silently to myself, to try to remember my favourite nursery rhymes – cosy childhood things.

But Rocco's voice was like a drill boring into my head – it wasn't very easy to ignore him. I don't know how old he was – maybe thirty. He was fit and lean. He wore combats and a grey T-shirt, and his hair was cropped short, like a real soldier's. When I tuned in fully to what he was saying, he was deep into a rant about people like me and my father and why he hated us.

'Your father is a traitor. He betrayed us. He and his friends robbed me and people like me – the real people of this island. He robbed us of our birthright. He's doing OK. And you, in your posh school. I hate you.'

I tried to avoid catching his eye, but I didn't want him to think I was ignoring him either, so I gave little glances in his direction. He was getting more and more agitated and less and less in control of himself. It was starting to feel very threatening, stuck in a room with this madman.

'This is my country, do you hear? It doesn't belong to the blacks or the yellows or the pinks or to you. But your filthy, rotten, no-good father sold it to the highest bidder. You people sicken me, in your fancy houses in your Citadel. I'd dash out all your brains and cut you into little pieces given half a chance. Believe me.'

I did believe him. I should have been terrified and I was terrified, but I wasn't overcome by terror. My heart froze when I heard the hatred in his voice and it hardened me against him. I wasn't going to show him any sign of fear or weakness. Stay strong, I told myself. Honour your father, I told myself. Your mother loves you, I told myself.

I started to play a game that our maid Francesca had taught me when I was little. I began to visualise the most outlandish thing I could imagine happening to Rocco. I imagined there was a bird building her nest on Rocco's head. I smiled to myself. It's a good trick, makes the other person seem ridiculous, makes you feel stronger. Soon the nest was full of little birdies and the whole family were perched right on top of his big head. The more I thought about it, the more foolish and ridiculous he seemed. The more he spoke, the more the nest rocked and bobbled on his big egg-head. OK, so it's stupid, but the point was, it made me feel a lot better. You have to have tricks like that to keep you sane in desperate situations.

'Our patriots died for this country. They didn't die so that the likes of you could rob it from the rest of us. Mark my words, we won't let you spoil it. We'll drive out everyone who contaminates it – everyone, do you hear?'

I glanced again in his direction. He was inching nearer and nearer. I noticed the muscles on his arms, and his pecs, just like the jocks in school. I wondered if he thought it was his patriotic duty to work out – keep fit for the nation.

I went on concentrating on the bird's nest.

'You think I'm horrible, don't you? Less than human. But I'll tell you something. I'm fighting for all the Tribe, all our people who have been banished beyond the Great River, while your father lets in any Tom, Dick or Harry who can pay.'

I had begun to feel differently about my parents, yes, but I couldn't help thinking he had a point about the people-who-could-pay bit. But I knew I mustn't allow myself to start thinking like that or I'd be all Stockholm syndrome in no time, drooling over my captors.

By this stage, Rocco had worked himself into a fury and just at the point when I thought things were going to get really nasty, Pippa Petersen decided to rejoin the world of talk and action. She stood up and placed herself between Rocco and me.

'Stop it,' she said. 'Stop saying those things.'

I wish I'd had a camera to record the look on Rocco's face – the look of astonishment and disbelief. I could see the sneer about to form, but Pippa wasn't finished.

'Those people you killed yesterday were innocent. And who do you blame for that?'

Not for the first time, I was filled with admiration for Pippa. But what timing! That girl had this irrepressible wish to die! Zip it, Pippa, I told her in my mind, which is more or less what Rocco told her to her face.

'Sit down,' Rocco said. 'Sit down and shut up or so help me ...'

I jumped up and took Pippa by the arm.

'It must be time to make that phone call,' I said. 'I'm ready now,' which of course was a total lie, but it was what came out of my mouth and it seemed to remind everyone of why we were there in the first place: hostages, ransom, prisoners, guns ...

It worked like a charm, because the change that came over Rocco was immediate and visible. In a flash he transformed from menacing thug about to beat us to death to professional soldier carrying out the orders of his general.

'Wait here,' he said, and turned to leave.

Rocco hadn't reached the door when the sounds started: strange whooping calls, the kind I imagine exotic birds make in the Amazon rainforest during mating season, and drumming, insistent, rhythmic drumming, low at first and then louder and faster. The whooping increased, and when it seemed that the noise had reached fever pitch, the first shots rang out. We were under attack!

After that the building came alive, with shouting and orders and men running here and there. All manner of noises surrounded the old barracks – shouts and cries, whooping, drumming, gunfire – and bottles filled with lighted rags and petrol were hurled through the windows. They fizzled out, though. Must have been Badlands petrol.

Pippa and I ran out of our room and looked down

the stairs. Already some of the attackers were in the house. They were Africans and it didn't take a genius to figure out that they were here because of what had happened to the women and children.

We ran till we found a stairs and taking the steps two and three at a time, escaped to the top of the house. There was a series of rooms, empty for the most part and sad-looking with their peeling plaster and rotting walls. In one there was an ancient wardrobe, the most ginormous piece of oak furniture I had ever seen. How or why anyone hauled it up three flights of stairs is a mystery.

Without saying a word, Pippa and I flew to it and managed with some difficulty to open its ancient doors, half-hoping that behind fur coats we'd find a snowy wood and a lamppost. But we didn't. No coats. No way out. Still, it was roomy inside and as good or as bad a place to hide as anywhere else we'd seen. We pulled the doors behind us and made them as secure as we could. There was some kind of fretwork at the top of the wardrobe which let in a little air and light. Then we sat toe to toe, knee to knee, wrapping our arms around our legs, making ourselves as small and invisible as possible, our heads bowed and tucked in, praying silently to the God I kept insisting I didn't believe in, hardly daring to breathe.

We could hear the fighting. Sometimes it was like the roaring of a sea, a great muffled thunder that gathered all the individual sounds and rolled them into one. And then there'd be a shout or the crack of a gunshot, or a blood-curdling scream. The sounds ran around the house, spitting and crackling and then dying away so that it was almost silent. We held our breath. One, two, three, four, five, six, seven, eight...

We were just beginning to hope that it was safe when we heard the faint but unmistakeable sound of footsteps moving quickly, running, getting closer, and then other footsteps following. The first footsteps, frantic and loud, came closer and then seemed to come right into our room. We held our breath again and closed our eyes. Someone began to fumble at the wardrobe doors. They were jammed shut, but it wouldn't take a strong man long to open them. We braced ourselves.

By this time the other footsteps seemed closer and then there was a cry, followed by a gunshot, a scream from the person on the other side of the wardrobe door and a yelp of triumph from his pursuer. We heard a body hitting the floor, inches from us. Then the footsteps moved on, away from our room.

OK, now, this bit is hard to explain because it doesn't really make sense, if you judge things on the basis of everyday reasoning and sense-making, which is, understandably, what most people do and it works fine for them. But this wasn't your average situation. I mean, when was the last time you sat on the floor of an ancient wardrobe in an abandoned barracks, while a gunfight raged, and waited for a person unknown to open the door of your hiding place and almost certainly be the cause of your death? And then heard this person being shot and crying out before he died inches away from you?

I was sitting, knees drawn up, head tucked down, toes touching Pippa's, petrified, my heart in my mouth, protected by two big old wooden doors, with someone on the other side trying to prise them open, to escape his pursuers and expose us to mortal danger.

The situation was not natural: it was super-, trans-, preter-, freaky-natural. Time stood perfectly still. Then there was this moment, this sublime, beautiful moment of total and complete silence, before the explosion that was the bullet being fired, propelled, sent screaming from the chamber of the gun.

I need you to stay with me on this one, because this is the really, really freaky part. And here is where I make a little confession. My school career in maths and science has not been a distinguished one. In fact, it has been nothing short of disastrous. This was a shame because my maths and science teacher was adorable and, poor man, he did try his best to help me understand some of the rudiments of time and the measurement of same, with cutesy little experiments using pendulums and hourglasses. Mr Hennessey waxed lyrical, in his sexy Scottish accent, about time being a dimension and how scientists could now measure time to the smallest, teeniest, weeniest part of a second, right down, in fact, to milli-, micro-, nano-, pico-seconds. He got so excited about the whole thing, all of which was to no avail, because I just didn't get it – until I heard the gunshot.

OK, this is my account of what happened, take it or leave it. The bullet that killed the man on the other side of the wardrobe – the man whose death almost certainly saved our lives – passed through him and entered the wardrobe. I saw it come towards me. Yes, I repeat, I saw the bullet coming towards me through the solid wooden doors of the vast, ancient wardrobe. Yes, I am saying that time slowed to a crawl and the bullet travelled in pico-, femto-, atto-seconds. I am saying I saw it come through the wooden panel of the door and head in my direction. I am saying that I saw, repeat, saw it enter my body. And in that atto-moment, I saw everyone I loved and said goodbye to them and told them I loved them, and I wasn't rushed for time, and then I died. (Didn't I?)

The fascinating thing about living your life in atto-seconds is that there's no hurry. Things happen slowly, atto-second by little atto-second. Oh, look, here is a bullet coming through the wood of the wardrobe door. Hi, it says, I'm coming your way.

Here I was, watching it travel through space, estimating where it would hit me, and I tried to make myself smaller, shrink into myself. And there I was looking at Pippa and smiling in the dim light of the wardrobe, doing my very best to reassure her that everything was going to be all right – not with any great conviction, I might add, for the aforementioned reason that I could see the bullet heading for me, but I didn't want Pippa to suffer on my behalf.

But I couldn't help her. She understood what was happening and she was beside herself with grief and love and horror and fear. And then the bullet disappeared into me and reappeared on the other side, smashed through the back of the wardrobe and burrowed (I suppose) into the wall. I took a sharp breath, I closed my eyes and, as far as I could determine, I died.

I'm now dead, so I'm not in a position to recount what effect my death had on poor Pippa, but I can imagine. You must remember that she was in fear of her life from the same people who shot the unknown man on the other side of the wardrobe and who, unwittingly, appeared to have shot me too. So she wasn't in a position to burst into tears, take me in her arms – all the things she would have done if things had been half-normal. (Though, come to think of it, under what circumstances would anyone consider getting shot to be normal?)

So Pippa covered her mouth with her hand and forced it closed. She had to keep quiet. She had to control herself, master her emotions. She sat there, frozen, every muscle strained and taut, listening, listening, hearing the footsteps move away and then dying out. In the end, there was nothing, no noise, except the sound of her heart beating.

Unfortunately I didn't keep a diary during my time in the other world. So here are the things I thought when I was dead, or as many of them as I can remember.

Pleasant Memories

Pippa telling me she knew I loved her

Damian comforting me when I was sad (and lying on his bed, in his room)

Me comforting him when he was in the sick bay at Sandybrook

The chat I had with my mother in her room a few days after the ball

Dad introducing me to the movers and shakers at the reception for the New Zealand delegation

John making me feel welcome in the Valley of the Thrushes

Holding the little boy in my arms
Seeing Joshua dressed like a peacock at the reception
for the New Zealand delegation
Meeting Cordelia

Regrets
Not making more of an effort to be nice to Mum
Not making more of an effort to be nice generally
Not asking Dad more questions about things
Not seeing Mattie

Feelings
So alone it's hard to describe and sad beyond words

Promises
God (OK, OK, you're there), if you give me one
more chance at life, I promise I will be a better person
and a more responsible person and I won't take things
for granted and I'll give up shoe shopping ...

It was the last thought that brought me to my
senses. Wait a minute, I told myself, there's no way
you're dead if you're thinking about shopping! That's
way too worldly. Get over yourself and open your eyes.

Which is what I did, feeling more than a little
sheepish and embarrassed and foolish. The first thing
I saw was Pippa, slumped down, her head on her knees,
her eyes shut tight, sobbing soundlessly to herself.

'It's OK,' I said. 'I think they're gone.'

Well, I won't bore you with the hugs and the Oh-my-Gods and the I-thought-you-were-deads and the general elation and clinging to each other in hysterical happiness and relief. We laughed and we cried and we hugged each other and then we laughed some more and cried some more and hugged some more.

When we settled down and composed ourselves we did a post-post-mortem.

'I thought you were dead,' Pippa said again, and because I was feeling somewhat guilty and a tad sensitive on the subject I thought I detected a note of accusation in her tone.

'I thought so too,' I said.

Pippa beamed a smile and I knew we were OK with each other. That's when I inspected my sweater and, lo and behold, there were the two holes where the bullet passed through. My little brain began to think and I put together the pieces of the jigsaw. So here's my explanation for what happened in the wardrobe.

To begin with, I hadn't eaten properly for a few days. Before that I'd been living with the Pilgrims and eating the purest of pure foods, which meant, in effect, no chocolate had passed my lips for a ridiculously long time and so my regular, skinny, flat-chested self was even more attenuated than usual. Moreover, I was wearing Mattie's sweatshirt, which was big on me to begin with and was now flapping around me like a sail. And I was sitting sideways-on to the front of the wardrobe, so that there was a lot less of me to hit than if I had been sitting facing the doors.

And so, when the fatal bullet passed through its first victim and carried on through the wardrobe doors, it entered through one side of my sweatshirt and exited the other without, in fact, injuring me. Unfortunately, my eyes saw otherwise and sent a signal to my brain, and my brain did what any self-respecting brain would have done in similar circumstances: it sent out an SOS to my nervous system to the effect that I was holed and taking water and would soon sink to the bottom of the ocean and rest in peace for ever and ever. Amen.

And such was the power of autosuggestion, I did fall into a death-like swoon. Which, fortunately, did not last. All of which is a totally rational way of explaining how I escaped death. However, another explanation, the one I favour, which I admit, lacks rationality, and may make you scoff, is that Mattie's sweater saved me. It was my magic cloak. I was alive and grateful. I wanted to live and do something good with my life. I was changing, I hope for the better.

So now you know. And then I pinched myself just to make sure I was really alive and then we decided to get out of the wardrobe and see how things were.

26

Outside the wardrobe we found Gorilla Boy lying on his back, his hand up in what may have been a gesture of surrender. His head rested in a small halo of blood. He had a startled look on his face, as if he was amazed that anyone would want to kill him; amazed that a bullet could really take your life away, and indignant, too. It was more than ironic that Gorilla Boy's death had probably saved Pippa and me.

I didn't feel or think any of the things I thought I would. I didn't think he'd gotten what he deserved. I didn't think, Live by the sword, die by the sword. Nor was I horrified or upset. I just saw a young man who should have been alive and was dead, so obviously and unambiguously dead, that there was no point in trying for a pulse. I can't quite say I felt sorry it was him, except in so far as you would feel sorry that any human being should die a violent and early death. If somebody had to die, I have to admit I would think, better him than anyone else.

I said a prayer for him (I'm getting good at that) and then we tiptoed down the stairs. That's where we found the next body. It was the young man with the kind voice, the one with the imaginary sisters, who sent Gorilla Boy away after the rat incident. This time I did feel sorry, really sorry. My God, this country was in an awful mess if young men were being mown down in this way. My father was going to have to hear about this.

Pippa said we should check to see if there was any sign of life. I nodded, not because I had any intention of touching the dead or almost-dead body, but because I knew it was the right thing to do even if I wasn't going to do it.

Pippa did it. She crouched down and felt for a pulse. Then she shook her head.

The front door was open. We hesitated. I'm not sure what we were waiting for.

'Do you think the general and Rocco survived?' Pippa asked.

I didn't know the answer and I wasn't about to search the house to find out. But if they had survived, chances were they'd be back soon enough looking for us. That's what galvanized us into action. We were determined to go through that door and get as far away from here as possible.

But before we did, we ran into the general's office where, only an hour or so before, we'd had tea and I grabbed the biscuits that were left and Pippa and I drank what little milk was there and we laughed, we actually laughed (hysterically, I suppose), because we were alive when we could so easily be dead. And then we ran out the door into whatever awaited us.

It was early afternoon so we had a good fix on east and west and clearly we wanted to head east, because that's where home lay – on the far side of the Great River and the Amber Zone. It's important to have goals and to feel that you are heading in the right direction, even if you are basically lost and screwed, which we were.

So we headed due east which brought us around the back of the house and we ran hard and fast and for as long as we could, which, in the case of Pippa Descendant-of-the-Norse-gods Petersen might have been miles, but in the case of Super-spoiled-little-rich-kid-driven-everywhere-by-my-chauffeur me wasn't very long. We ran through these amazing, badly neglected, dilapidated gardens which must have been fantastic in their day, seeing as how they registered on my consciousness even as I was running for my life. Then we hit upon some wooded fields and we stopped for breath and I realised just how unprepared we were for any kind of stay in the open. We had no blankets, no water, no food, no matches, no jackets. And this was in addition to all the other stuff we didn't have, like soap and shampoo and toilet paper. It might have made sense to head back to the barracks and grab what we could find, but there was no way I was going anywhere near it, as you can imagine. So, given our lack of preparation, our hope lay in one or many of the following happening:

(a) We meet some nice kind soul who is willing to help us

(b) We interrupt a teddy bears' picnic and are invited to join them (OK, yes, hysteria had set in)

(c) A wolf comes along and directs us to Granny's house (see above re: hysteria)

(d) A troop of our soldiers find us

(e) Mattie rescues us

(f) It doesn't rain or get too cold

(g) We outsmart, outrun and outfight any pursuers (possibly more hysterical an idea than all the rest put together).

I leaned against a tree and gasped for breath and generally waited until my head and my body seemed to be reunited, and then we set off at a brisk pace that was not too punishing. Given the circumstances, the forced walk along paths that were still serviceable was almost pleasant. There were no horrible midges to bite and bother us and the birds were singing and chirruping. After about an hour we reached a paved road that we guessed was headed in more or less the right direction, and although we debated the pros and cons of staying hidden, in the end we followed the road.

It was our mild season. Not cold but not too hot either. There were hedgerows on either side of us but the sun was shining on our heads and we were walking as fast as we could and scanning all around for any sign of danger. Before too long, my mouth was dry and I really, really wanted a drink of water and I think a form of post-traumatic stress overcame me because I felt my tongue swell in my mouth and I began to panic because I couldn't swallow.

When Pippa asked what was wrong, I mumbled something and pointed to my mouth and she came and looked inside. And then she put a spot of saliva on her little finger and ran it around the inside of my mouth, which may sound gross or weird but it actually worked. I no longer felt that my tongue was too big for my mouth and that I was going to choke or die. Which I suppose was a relief but I was suddenly overcome by a different feeling – one of complete and utter exhaustion.

I sat on the side of the road and clutched my knees and held on. I was not going to move until I was good and ready. I went back to being my four-year-old self and was ready to throw a tantrum if necessary. Pippa got the whole girl-on-the-verge-of-a-tantrum vibe and didn't try to rouse me. She sat down too, speaking quietly, saying we'd take a little rest and then continue and if I was too tired, we'd find a hiding place until I felt ready to resume our journey. So there we were, two lost girls sitting on the side of the road, scared and lonely and very, very tired.

I tried to stay positive. I did a checklist of good things in my life: the people I was returning to, the people I carried with me. I was trying out as many positive psychological tricks as I could when something miraculous happened: a beautiful, kind soul came along who was willing to help us.

Actually it was three kind souls. Three children. A boy of about ten, who was carrying a woven pannier on his back, filled with sticks. He was dreamy and smiley and seemed to float through the world rather than walk on it. He was dressed in a white tunic, shorts and leather sandals and I guess if there is a style of clothes for young angels walking among mortals, then he had it. He was accompanied by a girl who was a little older, maybe twelve, wearing a red dress that was wrapped around her and ankle bracelets that jangled as she walked. I'm not that well up on angelology but if there are male angels and female angels, then she was definitely another angel with the best angelic smile, maybe even the most beautiful I'd ever seen. Our female angel held the hand of a small boy of about three, whose big eyes peeped out from an orange knitted hat.

They stopped.

We smiled.

They smiled.

The smallest boy held out his hand. I took it. I stood up. Pippa stood up. The boy started walking. We started walking.

We went with the angels.

We walked at a leisurely pace. We didn't speak very much but it was a relaxed, friendly silence. After half an hour we veered off the road down a small laneway between the hedgerows. We heard the sounds and smelled the cooking before we saw the settlement. The 'village' was an abandoned farmhouse with outbuildings to which had been added some makeshift huts and tents. In the centre of the farmyard there was a fire with an enormous cooking pot, where three women sat preparing vegetables. One of the women was ancient, and I mean ancient, as if she had been cooking for a millennium.

They all looked up. They didn't seem surprised to see two pale newcomers waltzing into their farmyard. All three wore bright scarves, long skirts and colourful tops. A few small children played around. The boy with the pannier added the wood to a pile of kindling stacked neatly in the yard. So even in the Badlands people did normal things like cook meals and gather firewood. Nearby, there were two enormous dogs, yellowy like lions, that sniffed and looked in our direction with a fierceness that was absent in everyone else. I hesitated when I saw them, because I don't do the whole dog thing, but Pippa laughed and my little guide steered me towards the tents.

A young woman appeared. She was tall and seriously beautiful – not Sarah Flicker or the West Shopping Centre kind of beauty, but the real thing. She was also seriously pregnant and looked like the baby might pop out at any moment. She wore a bright red shawl over a gold dress. Boy, those people knew how to do colour. I wasn't sure how they reckoned beauty and social status in that little community, but that woman looked pretty regal to me. My little guide let go my hand and hugged her, though his head only reached her waist. She ruffled his hair.

'You are welcome,' she said, in perfect English. 'Please,' and she stood to the side and gestured for me to enter a tent. I looked to Pippa, but she shook her head.

'I think she wants you, Val. You're the princess here, remember.'

There she went again. I didn't much like that kind of talk. But the woman gestured for me to enter and there was something in the gesture that suggested urgency, so in I went. There was another child inside, lying on a mat, wrapped in a black and silver shawl. She was whimpering like a scared little puppy. I'm no good at guessing the ages of children but I reckon this little girl was less than two years old.

'She is very sick. Please, can you help her?' The woman spoke directly to me.

What could I say? I can't help. I'm just a skinny teenager with basic training in first aid. I can't possibly help you.

Well, clearly that wasn't an option, was it? But what could I do? Short of working a miracle, not very much. At the same time, I couldn't just stand there like a stick and do nothing. I wanted to help.

So here's what I did. I imagined what Pippa would do if she were me. I knelt down, loosened the shawl and touched the little girl's cheek, which was burning up, and touched her forehead which was hot and damp. I looked around. There was a bowl of water and a ladle. I scooped up a little and drank a mouthful and then, imitating Pippa, touched my fingers to my moistened lips and stroked the little girl's face and forehead and made soft sounds that I hoped were soothing. Then I closed my eyes and prayed to my mother and my father and to God and to Mattie and to Saint John the Healer, and to anyone else I could think of. I prayed for the little girl.

It was cosy in the tent. The floor was covered in a soft green cloth and there were bright rugs all around. It was so snug in there and I was so tired that I lay down beside the child and snuggled into her and closed my eyes.

When I woke, it took me a minute to remember

where I was. I looked at the little girl, the one I'd been asked to help. She was sleeping peacefully and looked less feverish. Her mother, the young pregnant woman, was sitting on a large cushion.

'I think she's a little better now,' I said.

I knew it was nothing I'd done. It was just that the fever had broken.

The young mother came and knelt beside her daughter. She undid the shawl. The child shifted and settled back into her sleep. The mother touched the child's forehead. Then she sat back and put her face into her hands. When she removed them, she looked at me shyly.

'I knew you would save her,' she said.

'I did nothing.'

The young mother took my hands in hers and raised them to her lips and kissed them.

I did nothing. But that's how myths start.

27

It was this incident that fuelled the rumour that I, Princess Valentina, was a miracle worker with sacred hands. As if it wasn't bad enough having one saint in the family.

When I came out of the tent, it was evening and the sun had set. Pippa came over to me and we hugged. I told her what had happened but she already knew.

'Your fame goes before you,' she said.

On the one hand, it was irritating, but on the other hand, it made me feel very responsible. If people had this (misplaced) trust in me, I was going to have to start living up to their trust. Very sobering.

There were more people in the farmyard now, men and older boys. I think they had been working in the fields. We were a group of about sixteen who sat down to eat. The women served the food on boards laid on the ground near the cooking pot. The heat from the fire protected us from the chill of the evening. The oldest woman ladled the stew from the big pot. There was meat and vegetables and you could taste the onions and garlic and other spices that I didn't know the names of.

We ate from wooden bowls, or rather drank from wooden bowls, because there were no spoons, and we mopped up the leftovers with bread, and I don't think food has ever tasted so delicious, even if it came from a pot that looked like it hadn't been cleaned in decades and had bones sticking out of it.

Pippa and I were the guests of honour so we were served first and everyone waited until we'd tasted the food and expressed our appreciation before taking theirs. The young mother – Abibech, she told me her name was – sat beside me, and Brihen, the girl with the bangles on her ankle, sat next to Pippa. All through dinner people smiled and nodded at us and I felt completely at home among these strangers, these immigrants who the AOT wanted to drive from the island and who our army prevented from crossing into the Amber or Green Zones. Abibech told us they were an extended family who'd come from Ethiopia. Pippa spoke of Joshua and Abibech knew who he was.

'How is he?' she asked.

'Fine,' I said, giving my default response, before Pippa had a chance to say a word. I felt myself blush.

How could I have said that when last time I saw him he was lying slumped over the wheel of a jeep and the AOT were closing in? He might be dead now, for all I knew. Why didn't I say that, instead of my insipid 'fine'? I hope I said it because I didn't want to remind Pippa of the ambush. And there was also the matter of my own feelings of guilt that I was somehow responsible for what had happened. So in a spirit of atonement for not telling the truth to our hosts, I promised Abibech that I would help her family when I got back to the Green Zone. I added that my father was an important man in the government, just in case she thought it ridiculous that a fourteen-year-old girl might say such a thing. But she laughed at me.

'Everyone knows you, Princess Valentina; everyone.'

That made me blush again, partly, I confess, with pleasure, and partly because I thought, Oh shit, this whole princess thing is getting seriously out of hand. But what was the point of trying to explain that I was not a princess, only the daughter of the president?

After the meal, the men and older boys retired to the farmhouse and the women and children settled in the two big tents. It was like being back in Sandybrook House, the way the sexes were segregated.

Not that I was complaining. Pippa and I were happy to be among the women. There were lots of gossipy questions rattling round in my head, like: Was the father of the baby one of the men we'd seen at dinner? And if so, which one? Was Abibech married to him? I was less certain about Dabir, our little guide, being her child, though I knew that the little girl in the tent was hers. If we'd stayed another day, I'm sure all my questions would have been answered. That's how much at home I felt there that I could think such idle, silly thoughts.

Brihen got us to try on some shawls and dresses and we played dress-up and stood before a mirror to admire ourselves and see how good we looked in our borrowed robes. I refrained from cracking the joke about how Pippa looked like the kind of girl that an Ethiopian prince might desire. And in that sneaky way that sorrow has of creeping up on joy, the little happiness I felt in that tent with Brihen and Abibech was cast into shadow. Not even Dabir's smile could overcome my survivor's guilt at feeling happy and safe among friends when, for all we knew, Damian, Joshua and Thomas could be dead.

I asked to use the toilet. I needed some space and privacy. Much to my relief and satisfaction, the arrangements (I know, I know, I'm a bit obsessive about this kind of stuff, but that's me) were pretty good. There was an old toilet in the farmyard and the water still flowed into the cistern when you pulled the chain. (Yes, chain. It was an ancient contraption, but it worked.) So I visited the loo and thought my thoughts.

That's where I asked myself this question: could I return the hospitality of Abibech and her family at any time in the near future, and have them all visit my family? And if not, why? They were good people. Isn't that what hospitality is about – making people feel welcome? Responding to people in kind? Doing unto others what you hope they would do unto you? If any of our professed religion was taken seriously, then I was duty-bound to repay their kindness. And I would try my level best to do so.

That set me thinking about Pippa and her family and how they'd have to be allowed to stay in the Green Zone. It wasn't as if there were a million of them. There were only her parents, two brothers and her grandmother. By all accounts her father and brothers were pretty impressive in the scientific brain-cell department and her mother and grandmother were no slouches when it came to botany and animal husbandry. If ever a family was a candidate to run a model farm in a place like Sandybrook House, the Petersens were it.

See, that's what happens when you sit in the dark in a small room and think your thoughts. I might have been there a lot longer had not Dabir knocked on the door to see if I was still alive.

We slept in a heap on the floor. The two yellowy dogs sneaked in at some point in the night and lay next to me. And then I discovered something about myself which I'd never known. Dog fleas find me irresistibly attractive. They love me, adore me and, to prove it, they sucked my blood and feasted on me. Oh yes, I never felt so loved, so bitten and itchy and scratchy, with horrible red sores appearing like a rash on my legs and ankles. Some princess!

So I was not my usual sweet self when I woke in the morning. When Brihen saw the state of my legs, she prepared a white paste that eased the discomfort.

Abibech slept later than us. And when a handsome young man came to wake her, and I saw how tenderly he spoke to her, I knew he was the baby's father and the little girl's too. It was he who told us of the rumour that Rocco and the AOT were planning to strike back at those who had attacked the general and taken the two white girls.

I didn't need to be a genius to realise that Pippa and I had better clear off very soon and not put Abibech or her family in any danger on our behalf. I told her we would leave and she and some of the other adults consulted in their own language. That was how it was proposed that Pippa and I should travel through the Badlands to the Great River on a donkey, guided by Hakim, the oldest man in the family, and for our safety we would dress in shawls and long dresses.

We had a quick breakfast of fruit, said our goodbyes and hugged Brihen and kissed Abibech and Dabir and thanked everyone for being so kind to us and then we were rushed off to safety, though rushed is probably an exaggeration seeing as we travelled sitting on a donkey which Hakim led along at a steady pace. As I looked back at Abibech and her family for the last time, I vowed never to forget them and to keep my promise to them as best I could.

Since I'd left home, I was fast gathering people I felt a bond with. First there'd been the little boy and that poor sick family, then Cordelia and her family and now this little community. This is me, Valentina O'Connor, who until very recently hadn't a friend in the world – except Mattie. And speaking of friends, I began to wonder how Damian was. He wasn't exactly my dream boy any more, but he was my friend, and I loved him and I wanted him to be OK.

We weren't in another country travelling on the
donkey, we were in another age.

In the Badlands, petrol and other fuels were in short
supply. While we saw all kinds of mechanised vehicles,
most people walked or went on carts pulled by horses,
cows or donkeys. There were a lot of people in the
Badlands, way more than I imagined, and once we got
to the main road (more dirt road than the highways in
the Green Zone) there was a never-ending stream of
people headed east, as were we.

Hakim spoke no English and we spoke no Amharic
but that didn't prevent us from communicating
with smiles and nods and thumbs-ups. Hakim was
unflappable and his pace never varied. He looked back
at us at regular intervals and smiled encouragement
as he checked if we were OK and we continued on

our stately, sedate way. Given all that had happened to us, Hakim's manner and age were reassuring and I might have found the journey relaxing if the backbone of our donkey (whom we nicknamed Eeyore for his sad expression and hangdog look) had inflicted less suffering on my poor, delicate behind. It is not often that I long to have loads of fatty flesh on the bones of my bum, but that certainly was one of those times.

The multitudes of the earth passed us. This was the world after the flood but we were on dry land, and it seemed that people from all over the globe had converged here.

People were dressed in clothes that I'd never seen in the shopping malls of the Citadel. And get this: we saw people go by on camels – actual, live, breathing, smelly (and farting, it must be said) camels. This was the original zoo of the new. (Deep poetry reference there. Ms Parkinson, our English teacher, would be proud of me.)

So, apart from the old reliables dragging me down, which I won't bother enumerating yet again, our epic donkey trek was a veritable feast of colour and randomness and Pippa and I devoured it. We were in the Badlands, right smack bang in the middle of things, on an ass, in disguise, and it was exhilarating. We could see a different way of life developing before our eyes – food and animals being traded and sold. This was what I had come to learn about.

All right, I know that's a rewriting of history but we were there and we did see with our own eyes what life was like beyond our borders, which is more than the vast majority of our citizens have seen or are likely to see in their lifetime. So, yes, I felt some kind of accomplishment. And next time Damian (alive Damian) tried to play his expert-on-the-Badlands card, I'd trump him. It's good to have high and noble aspirations.

We reached the town, only it was more of a shanty town than a real town. As far as the eye could see, there were shacks built on stilts, and the reason for that was soon pretty obvious. About the same time as the town came into view, so did the Great River, which was ten times – no, twenty times – wider than I'd imagined. Many of the shacks were in the water. Pippa said the river was proof of what Damian had told us weeks before about the earthquake in Greenland and the ice tipping into the sea. The Great River was tidal and the sea had swelled it so much that the banks had burst along its full length. I could hardly bear to look at Pippa because I could see in her agonised expression what she was thinking.

The hundreds and thousands of shacks were extraordinary creations, ungainly like flamingos and made out of an assortment of the most random materials; anything, in fact, that came to hand: wood, yes, but also bits of metal, plastic, drums, sacks, tarpaulin, sheets, rags, leather, corrugated iron. You name it and we saw it. Some of the shacks looked flimsy; others were solid and some were built as neatly and cleanly as any architect-designed building in the Citadel.

To go with the makeshift town, there was a makeshift harbour and a food and clothes market. There were also people in small boats selling various things, including chickens and small animals. It was bedlam. Near the water's edge, Hakim signalled us to get down and he tied up the donkey and made it clear that we were to stay there while he went off to find someone to bring us across the river.

Standing there beside our little donkey, surrounded by people who did not disguise their curiosity, but looked us over as if we were for sale – which, come to think of it, we might have been, if the sale of young women was part and parcel of that world as I suspected it might have been (though maybe that's just my prejudice, or my deepest fear, breaking through) – was not exactly my idea of having fun. We watched the passing world and spoke little to each other, not wanting anyone to know where we came from.

Northwards, up the river, there was an enormous dump, partly covered by the flood waters. Gulls and ugly black birds circled and squawked and dived down. When the breeze blew from that general direction, the stench was unbearable. The other thing we noticed was the mud: thick, smelly, and squelchy underfoot. I was glad we were not barefoot. The river was a road, a sewer, a dump and a graveyard too, and we saw some pretty unpleasant stuff caught in the current of its brown, gloopy water. All along the bank of the river there were dogs – skinny, fearsome, avid creatures who pulled things out of the flow and fought over carcasses and God knows what. Had they not had such rich pickings, they might have smelt my fear and turned on me.

Maybe because of the smell I thought of Mouldy Old Bowels and made a mental note to inform him that the great monastic settlement that we had studied in history, and which he had described as 'a shining light in the darkness of an ignorant age,' was marooned far out in the flood water and looked forlorn and lost, which was pretty much how I felt now that the euphoria of being in the Badlands was wearing off and the stench of the river began to overpower me.

Hakim reappeared. He had assembled a small group of followers who looked at me as if I was an exhibit in a museum – exhibit A, the young girl with the healing hands who is known as Princess Valentina. Aaagh!

They stood around me, staring blankly, not catching my eye or not acknowledging me if they did. It was damn hard to keep my composure and act with the sweet grace of a princess and miracle-worker or whatever the hell I was supposed to be when all I wanted to do was lash out at the next pair of staring eyes. Not for the first time, I was grateful to Pippa, who acted as a human shield and planted herself before me.

So it was a big relief when a man who might have been Hakim's twin stepped forward and made it known that he would bring us across the river. That gave a lift to my spirits, all the more so when I saw an old signpost pointing the way towards the capital. We were going home. The lift to the spirit took a bit of a nosedive when Pippa and I saw the 'boat' that was to bring us across to the other side of this fast-flowing, treacherous, soupy-brown open-sewer of a river. It was a small, wooden flat-bottomed boat, the kind you see little old Asian ladies using to sell fruit and vegetables in floating markets. It was pretty, ideal for a romantic adventure in a garden pond, but scary for crossing what we had to cross, namely the hateful, detestable River Styx.

The whole assembly, which had grown and multiplied, was standing there, nodding and smiling and bowing, a whole guard of honour, and I did my best to keep my end of the princess thing going when all I wanted to do was throw up and get away from the stench as fast as I could. So it was almost a relief to get on board our little vessel and set out for the other side.

29

Two young girls and one old man in a small boat on a big river. Pippa was perched in the front of the boat, the boatman sat in the back and I was piggy in the middle. Pippa and I were both on high alert. We pulled our shawls tight around our heads and scanned for danger and willed the boat to go faster and cross safely. We zigzagged to avoid the other boats, the majority of which were navigating parallel to the shore, and tried to catch the current, not row against it, because the little boat was not made to ride the swell. Our boatman, Hakim's twin, whose name I never knew, pulled gently on the oars and we seemed destined to travel as sedately on water as we'd travelled with Hakim on land. So, much as we wanted to go faster and get to the other damned side of the river, our little boat meandered as slowly as a donkey.

Then a motor launch came round the bend at speed. We heard the high rev of the engine before we saw it. We both gasped at the same moment, when we recognised Rocco standing in the prow, his machine-gun slung from his shoulder. That boat was not for changing course or giving way to the traffic on the river. No sir, this was testosterone-fuelled power on full throttle. These were the lords of the river patrolling their territories, so the whole flotilla of small boats, which was on probably the busiest stretch of the entire river, scattered in all directions before the masters of the universe and, just to be sure that everyone got the message, Rocco took the gun from his shoulder and fired off a round of shots.

It might have been laughable in a surreal kind of way, except these jocks had guns and we knew what they were capable of doing. This show of force was intended to send a message to anyone who thought Rocco and the AOT had been put out of business by yesterday's attack on the old barracks where we'd been held.

Weren't we, the State of Free Citizens, supposed to have anti-terrorist units and border patrols? Where the hell were they when we needed them?

Maybe because we were navigating across the river and moving so slowly, or maybe because it looked as if we had ignored their warning, Rocco's launch seemed to single us out for special treatment and aimed itself in our direction. Obviously, a motor-powered high-speed launch can travel a whole lot faster than a small rowing boat with an old man pulling on the oars. Rocco and his crew were on top of us in no time.

The back of the boat took the brunt of the collision. We were spun like a spinning top and for an atto-second, I thought a spot of dizziness was the worst that would happen to us, until I felt the water rising up and realised with a sharp, sudden shock that we were sinking fast. No, I thought. I can't have survived a bullet aimed at my heart (I'm allowing myself some poetic licence) and escaped from the AOT to end up drowning in a stinking river. That's SO unfair. I shook my metaphorical fist at God, while with my real hands I tried to unwrap myself from the layers of clothes Brihen had given us to wear.

Here's the thing. When I was in the wardrobe and the bullet came through the doors, everything happened in slow time. On the river, after the boat was more or less cut in two, everything happened in fast-forward mode. I did have my colourful wrap unravelled and it's just possible that the air caught the material and filled it like a parachute which kept me afloat for few vital seconds or this may have been wishful thinking on my part. In any case, the worst of all nightmares occurred then: I went under.

'Don't swallow any water, whatever you do!' Pippa shouted as the boat sank, and I immediately clamped my jaws shut so forcefully, it gave me a pain in my face.

The next bit is clearly psychotic but that doesn't mean it wasn't real. In fact, it was the most vivid of all the things that had happened since we were kidnapped. Underwater, I saw dead people who'd been dumped in the river, old and young, born and unborn, their mouths opening and closing like fish. There were carcasses of animals – rats and giant fish tore strips of rotting flesh from their bones. I struck out at anyone or anything that came next or near me and thrashed maniacally, resisting the urge to breathe even though my lungs were fit to burst. I went totally berserk down there where the fishes live.

However, amazingly, I somehow propelled myself to the surface and stuck my head high enough to breathe in some air ('fresh' would be pushing it) without swallowing a mouthful of the vile water.

Even better was the sight of Pippa's head stuck similarly high in the air. We looked like a pair of seals treading water. Of our boatman and our boat there was no sign. A truly good person would have been devastated that our Good Samaritan was missing, and of course I was sorry that our boatman had gone under, but I confess that just at that moment, my selfish little mind was filled with trying to figure out how we'd get safely out of the river and not fall back into the hands of 'Give me fifteen minutes alone with Blondie there' or his general or any of their friends.

So it was with a sinking feeling that I heard a motor boat getting closer. And then Pippa and I were fished out of the river and dumped unceremoniously on the floor of a boat. There were shades of the helicopter incident and I was waiting for a fat oaf to stand on my head and grunt and groan and speak in Gorilla, but none of that happened. Instead, a pair of hands wrapped each of us in a blanket and helped us upright and the boat headed for the Amber shore.

We had been rescued. By the Good Guys; the real – as opposed to the pretend – border guards. I started to cry, which was not as big a dent to my pride as it might have been because the intrepid Pippa did the same.

When we were finished crying with relief, Pippa remembered our boatman and asked the guard who attended us if they had found him. When he said no, we requested that they turn the boat, which was some kind of fancy, high-speed pursuit craft, and he conferred with his superior who agreed to do a sweep before landing.

I suddenly hated the idea of heading away from the Amber shore and encountering the AOT for a fight in the middle of that stinking cesspool of a river. When I voiced my concerns over that possibility, the young officer in charge explained to us, his two frightened passengers (who, incidentally, were also wet, stinking and shivering) why there was no danger of a confrontation with the AOT. But he spoke in

Army, so I only got the gist without understanding the finer points of 'the rules of engagement'.

At that point I revealed that we had been held hostage by the AOT and had only escaped because they had been attacked by a group of immigrants. If, I suggested, Rocco realised who had been fished out of the river, the 'rules of engagement' might not, in fact, govern this situation.

Well, as you can imagine, my announcement had quite an effect. For starters, the officer turned a whiter shade of pale and swallowed hard.

'You were held hostage by the AOT?'

Now that the penny had dropped, I watched him as he processed this piece of information. I could see him thinking, Who are these girls that the AOT would hold them hostage? so I told him who we were. He looked at me, trying to see the president's daughter beneath my disguise.

'Good Lord,' he said, shaking my hand and then, remembering himself, saluted me.

It seemed that he had not been out searching for us, which I thought odd, because I had imagined our disappearance would be the talk of the island. Then I remembered my row with Damian about how the government controlled the news. Maybe we were not making the headlines after all? But then another, more disturbing thought came to my mind: what if nobody knew we were missing? It was possible that

John thought we were still off doing our exercises in the mountains, that he hadn't realised that anything had happened to us. But was it possible that no one had discovered the crashed jeep? No, that was in the Green Zone. Someone must have seen it.

Of course it was known we were missing. But known by whom? Did my father know? Was he, at this moment, berating John for allowing us to go? Was he amassing an army and getting ready to invade the Badlands? Or was he sitting in his study reading his briefing papers as if nothing had happened? Had he told Mum? If he had, what was she doing?

The young officer coughed to attract my attention. Then he requested that we head straight for the shore where we would be escorted as quickly as possible to the Green Zone. And, he added, he would radio for another boat to conduct a search for our missing colleague. I thought to correct him and tell him that Hakim's twin was not a 'colleague', just a kind old man who believed I was someone worth losing his life for. But I knew he had to be dead, lost in that horrible underworld.

I looked back to the far side of the river, to the shanty town teeming with people who had fled to our island to escape fires and floods. And look at them now, living in fear of being washed away or attacked, not to mention the diseases and sickness that the river carried.

To many of them I was a miracle-worker, a princess, someone in whom they placed their hopes and dreams. So I told the officer we would gladly accept his proposal and, to a spontaneous round of applause from the six soldiers on the boat, we sped away from the Badlands.

The young officer introduced Pippa and me to the five other soldiers in his command. They were all kind and open, and they asked if Pippa and I would pose for photos. They didn't seem to mind that we were stinking and wet and bedraggled, so we did and they seemed to think it an honour. If only it was so easy to make everyone happy.

I knew from what he said that the officer was hoping he and his unit would have the further honour of escorting us back to the Green Zone and receiving whatever Boy Scout badges they hand out for finding a lost daughter of the president. Well, I wasn't going to rain on his parade and so I said the honour would be ours, which seemed to go down pretty well with the boys.

Their boat was kept at a heavily fortified dock on the river and once it was safely stowed, we loaded into an army van (not, I hasten to add, the mode of transport I would have chosen) and set off at speed across the Amber Zone. Pippa and I sat in the cab between the driver and the officer, whose name was Gerry, and though it was a bit of a squeeze, there was none of the funny stuff that had so amused Gorilla Boy. Anyway, after what had happened the last time we rode in the back of an army van, the one disguised as an ambulance, I was happier to sit up front.

The Amber Zone looked pretty normal to me, with hardly any immigrants to be seen and members of our tribe going about their lives. That made me wonder why the Amber Zone was not fully integrated into the State of Free Citizens – another question I needed to ask my father. And there was one thing bugging me that I needed to ask our young officer about his 'rules of engagement'. He had allowed the AOT to speed down the river terrifying all and sundry and I wanted to know why.

'Because the president forbids any action near to Newtown or any of the immigrant encampments along the river.'

Which meant that my father knew about these people and was concerned for them, to some degree. Well, that was a point in his favour. What else did he know, my father the Inscrutable? Then I realised the officer was waiting for me to say something, so I said the first thing that popped into my head.

'Where are you taking us?'

'To the border guard station at Rockford.'

'Could you take us to the station at Sandybrook?'

'Is that a good idea, Val?' Pippa asked. 'Remember Colonel MacDonald.'

'You know the colonel?'

'We met him once and it wasn't a pleasant experience.'

'The colonel was removed from office yesterday and is awaiting trial for treason,' the officer said.

'Treason?'

And then he became self-conscious as it dawned on him that this sudden action might have something to do with the colonel betraying me, the president's daughter, to the enemies of the state. Pippa told him that we were almost certain that's what he had done.

'What will happen to him if he's found guilty?' Pippa asked.

'The penalty for treason is execution.'

Creep though MacDonald might have been, I was not delighted at the prospect of another death. We had seen too many already in our short time out of the Green Zone. 'If the penalty is death,' I asked, 'why would he have done it?'

'I don't know. Maybe because he sympathises with the aims of the AOT, or because he hates your father and his policies on immigrants. Or maybe he doesn't want you to succeed to the presidency.' He looked a bit self-conscious as he said this.

'The presidency? Me succeed to the presidency? But that's ridiculous. My father is the president; he's not a king. And if he were a king, then one of his two sons would succeed him, not his youngest child who also happens to be a girl, in case you hadn't noticed.'

'I am aware you are a young lady, Miss Valentina.' Here he blushed. 'But it is widely believed that you are being educated to succeed your father as president of the State of Free Citizens.'

'That's why you're known as Princess Valentina,' Pippa added.

'That's very nice. But it's not true.'

'Everyone believes it's true,' the officer said.

I imagined a journey of fifty miles with the conversation consisting of 'Is true', 'Is not', 'It is so', 'It is not' and I didn't find this an awfully appealing prospect, so I brought us back to where we had started.

'So you could take us there – to Sandybrook House?'

'Yes.'

'OK. Let's go there.'

I sat back and looked down at myself. And my God, something had happened. Something amazing – I had developed breasts! I swear to God. Overnight, they had grown. OK, they weren't like the humps on a camel, or the pyramids. No, but if I can continue with my Arabian similes, they were like small sandhills in the desert. Not spectacular or too obvious but undeniably there and real. And I lay back in the seat and pretended to doze and pushed my breasts as far forward as I could.

We crossed the bridge on the River Nore which marked the boundary between the Amber and Green zones, and there was the usual inspection and whispered conversations before we sped to Sandybrook House. At the gates we were waved through and the van pulled up outside the front door. The young officer saluted and said it was an honour to have met us. I didn't bother with presidential protocol but gave him a hug and thanked him and then we fairly bounded up the steps to my new favourite house.

Cordelia came down the stairs, just like she'd done four days earlier when we first arrived. She was the same no-nonsense Cordelia, dressed in her blue summer dress.

'Oh, you poor dears,' she said when she saw our bedraggled state. Come on, follow me. I'll run two hot baths and find a change of clothes for you. You'll feel so much better when you're clean and freshened up and then we'll have tea.'

My bath was in the bathroom off our old room. I know I'd only slept in it for one night, but it felt like it was ours. Pippa was in another bathroom down the hall. This bath was the real deal, with gallons of water and soap suds and fragrant salts. It was luxurious.

Cordelia came in without knocking, and with no false modesty she took a pitcher and poured fresh water over my head and washed and rinsed my hair as if I were her baby sister or her daughter. She hummed away to herself and said next to nothing to me, except 'Tip your head back' and 'All done now'. Then off she marched and I hoped Pippa was about to get the same treatment from this mad old lady, who was, at that moment, the most wonderful woman in the world.

When I sank back into the bath, I made a resolution. Next time I was having a bath I'd ask Mum to come and wash my hair. (I knew it was never going to happen – come on, letting Mum see me naked? How likely was that? But the idea, the hypothetical idea, made me feel good all the same.)

When I got out of the bath, Cordelia had taken away all my stinking clothes and left me a clean set. The knickers were the biggest I'd ever seen, really old-fashioned, but brand new. I imagined a cupboard somewhere stacked to the top with big white knickers. The dress was sky-blue with little puffed sleeves and a flouncy skirt, so that I looked like Little Bo Peep. The shoes were slip-ons in patent leather and there were white ankle socks to go with them. Cordelia had even left me some of her perfume. When Pippa appeared a little later, she was dressed in almost an identical set of clothes. We looked comical, but pretty too, and we fitted right in with our surroundings. I was quite happy to play at being a little girl. I didn't think there would be too many opportunities in the future.

In the kitchen, Cordelia gave us tea and scones with butter and jam. Old Mrs Devereux was there and she ate slowly and looked slyly at us, as if we reminded her of someone from years before but she couldn't quite say whom. Daisy made an appearance and stood in the doorway of the kitchen smoking her non-existent cigarette.

'Aren't you the two young lovelies,' she said, before waltzing off up to her room.

Before we'd finished our scones the new commanding officer arrived to see us. He did not have a dead fish handshake and his uniform looked like a real uniform, not something to put on a tailor's dummy. He didn't tell me he was an old friend of my father's or try to ingratiate himself. In other words, he was everything that Colonel MacDonald was not. He was polite, businesslike and I trusted him immediately. He told me that the presidential helicopter was on standby to bring us home.

I should have been delighted, but I wasn't. I wanted to stay in Sandybrook House for a little longer and postpone returning to the Citadel because I knew instinctively that life would be different from now on. And there was the matter of seeing Mattie. I felt almost certain that he would make contact, so I asked Cordelia if we could stay the night and return first thing in the morning.

Mattie arrived around dinner time that evening. He was wearing combat fatigues and looked older and harder than I remembered him. Not that he didn't smile and kid me about my dress and give me an enormous big hug.

Then he gave Pippa a kiss on each cheek and treated her like his long-lost cousin.

'I've heard all about you from Joshua, who, incidentally, is making a good recovery from his accident, as indeed are your two friends.'

'So Damian is OK?'

Mattie smiled. 'He's doing well.'

Relief washed over me.

The mention of Joshua heightened Pippa's colour and made her act all bashful, which drew attention from me and my relief at hearing Damian was safe. I really wanted to know more details about how badly injured he was. However, the kitchen was a veritable hive of activity and I knew I would have to wait till later when Mattie and I had our real talk. In the meantime, I enjoyed watching Mattie charm everyone in sight. Pippa (naturally) fell immediately under his spell, which was exactly as it should have been. Anything less than total devotion on her part would have put a serious strain on our relationship. This is Mattie we're talking about.

Even Cordelia got a bit flirty, which was alarming to see, as she more or less neighed like a horse when Mattie said anything remotely (or even not remotely) funny. And Mrs Devereux seemed pleased by Mattie's coming, though I think she thought it was twenty years earlier and Mattie was her son, Will, come home for a holiday. It wasn't my place, or anyone else's, to tell her that he was never coming back. Daisy arrived in soon enough, and did her 'Hello darling' routine, but Mattie just said, 'Daisy! What will your visitors think?' and that was that.

Thereafter, Daisy acted like a little girl trying to please her favourite uncle, and Mattie coaxed her along so that our dinner passed off pleasantly enough, if you ignored the fact that the three Devereuxes thought of Mattie as three different people and spoke to him accordingly. I got the distinct impression that this was not the first time Mattie had visited Sandybrook House and eaten dinner with the family. So that was something else to include in our so-tell-me-what-have-you-been-up-to-since-I-saw-you-last pow-wow.

After dessert Cordelia, who was perfectly sane again and back to her no-nonsense self, suggested that Mattie and I might like to take our tea in the library and have our 'little chat'.

The library turned out to be a gorgeous room with high ceilings and long classical windows facing the pasture land. I'd say all that remained of the family's heirlooms were kept there, so that it looked like a room from a different house, a grand Italian palazzo, or the house the family lived in before the floods and the fires changed everything. No wonder they preferred to live in the past.

Mattie settled in an armchair, his legs spread before him, and lit a cigarette (a habit I find disgusting, but I was not going to spoil our reunion by coming over all moral on the tobacco question). He also poured himself a brandy from the decanter Cordelia had left for him (a habit I associated with old men but I did my best not to betray my feelings), while I drank a cup of tea from a china cup, an antique from the last century or two, but pretty, and nibbled on an oat biscuit. It was more than a little weird to be there, acting out scenes from someone else's life, from another lifetime, but acting our own lives too, even if we were disguised as Lucy and Mister Tumnus. (I do love that book.)

I won't lie and say that it was the most wonderful evening of my life because it wasn't, but I suppose that's what happens when you build something (or someone) up in your mind to be this great event, greater than it can ever be in reality. Here I was at last with Mattie, my hero, and I couldn't get beyond the fact that he wasn't the way I remembered him, all light-hearted, energetic and charming. No, somewhere along the way (and out of sight), he'd turned into a younger version of Dad (whom I love, don't get me wrong) with his brandy and cigarette (with Dad it's an occasional cigar) and a grown-up, serious way of looking into the fire. My Mattie had left the building but I missed his departure and I don't think he'll be back any time soon.

So there I was with my new Mattie, waiting to hear what had caused the change, though I already knew because I'd finally gone into the forest and met the wolf and knew it was kill or be killed in the forests of the night. That would harden anyone, myself included. I suppose if you were trying to do some good in the Badlands you might feel more than a bit overwhelmed and take an occasional glass of brandy to raise your spirits. But it's one thing understanding why something is the way it is and quite another accepting it. I wasn't exactly in a sulk but I suppose I resented the Badlands and all that went with it, because it meant that things could not go on as they had before, much as I might want them to.

After the chitchat and the little bit of family news and telling Mattie about my visits to the Valley of the Thrushes and John and Gwen, I told him everything that had happened to us since setting out with Joshua four days earlier. He listened attentively without interrupting me, and when I finished telling my story he sat for a long time staring into the fire and I saw that his eyes were tearful and he bit his lower lip. At last he looked at me and smiled a sad smile and said, 'I'm so sorry you went through all that.'

And then he answered some of my questions. Yes, there was a news blackout on my kidnapping. An elite force of anti-terrorist troops was assembled and was set to attack known strongholds of the AOT as soon as I was found safe and well (which meant there might well have been fighting in the Badlands, even as we spoke). Reports were that the general – Tadhg, with his tea and biscuits – had been killed in the attack by a group of armed immigrants.

But how did Mattie know all this? That was when I learned a whole lot of new things about his life. I'd always seen Mattie's disappearance as an act of rebellion, son against father, a defiant gesture of filial disobedience.

It wasn't. Dad and Mum had helped him. They hardly spoke about him because (1) they wanted to protect him and (2) they were heartbroken. So much for my position as the only one who really missed Mattie.

And then came the coup de grâce.

'It wasn't a brave thing, Val, going to work in the Badlands,' Mattie said. 'I ran away because I wasn't brave enough to stay and try to help Dad. See, it's easier to hide out there and pretend to be heroic and a rebel than to stay and do what he does – make hard choices. He knows that everyone fears him and not that many love him. He sent you here. He wanted you to know what things are like in the Badlands. You're the one he hopes will succeed him.

'Wait up, wait up. He sent me here? What are you saying, Mattie? Dad was behind all this?'

'Not the kidnapping, obviously.'

'Well, that's good to know.'

I sat there fuming. It's never nice being the last one to know something, especially something so obvious that you wonder how the hell you didn't see it before now. Of course Dad knew about my trip to the Badlands. He knows everything. There was, I now realised, no way that it would have been possible for me to go where I went without Dad knowing it. I was feeling a right idiot, though. I refused to look at Mattie and when I spoke, it was like a robot.

'So, what's all this about me succeeding Dad, Mattie?'

'That's the plan.'

'But what about the council? Father can't just decide who will be president.'

The council does what Father wants it to do. Let's face it: Dad is a benign dictator, Val. People want a strong leader in charge who will do what has to be done and that's what Dad has done for the past ten years. There'll be elections in five years' time but they're only a formality. I know you're angry, Val.'

'I've a right to be angry, Mattie. I've been treated like a fool and you were in on it. When was I going to be told that Dad was behind this whole thing?'

'When you got back. But then the kidnapping changed everything.'

'Too right it did. And why now? Why was it so important that I experience the Badlands first-hand if Dad's going to be re-elected in five years' time?'

'There's no guarantee.'

'You just said he can do anything he likes.'

At this point Mattie stood up and walked around the room and came back and stood by the fireplace.

'Dad will tell you this in his own good time when you get home, so don't let on I told you.'

'Told me what?'

'He's not well.'

'What do you mean, "He's not well"?'

'He has cancer.'

'Cancer?'

I was repeating everything Mattie said and watching myself from a great height sitting in a beautiful room talking about my father having cancer (oh my God) and possibly having no more than five years left to live. I was watching myself discuss the possibility that in five years' time I would be the only candidate in the presidential election and, like a good actress in a play, I got through all my lines and didn't break down.

'So, Damian, Pippa, Joshua, Thomas, John ... they were all in on the plan?' I asked now, instead of asking how Dad was, what kind of cancer, whether it could be treated. I just couldn't face all that right then.

'Joshua; not the others.'

'But Damian suggested we come,' I said.

'And Father took advantage of that suggestion.'

'And you did, too.'

'I wanted to see you, Val.'

'You could have come home.' I felt like crying. 'Who can I trust now, Mattie?'

'Yourself, Val. And everyone who loves you.'

'You lied to me. You all did.'

'We gave you a chance to see the world beyond the Green Zone.'

'Do I have a choice?'

'You can refuse, Val.'

'Like you refused?'

Mattie laughed. 'I was never Dad's choice. John neither, so we didn't have to choose.'

'Hold on. You're telling me that Dad chose me over you and John? Please. People think John is a saint and you're the Robin Hood of the Badlands. There's no way Dad chose me over either of you.'

'Dad trusts you, Val. Of the three of us, he thinks you are the one who can lead the state.'

'That's ridiculous.'

'Dad sees something in you that reminds him of himself. You're tough and you're practical. And you've always been his favourite; Daddy's little girl.'

I still couldn't understand. Mattie said it was because John was too soft and good and he himself was too stubborn when it came to matters of principle. Which pretty much sounded like I had been chosen because I was a hard-hearted, practical bitch who didn't believe in very much. It hardly sounded like a ringing endorsement of my character.

As you can imagine, I was pretty exhausted after this conversation with Mattie. There was a lot to take in. The worst bit was about Dad being sick. Worse than sick – there was the possibility he might die sooner rather than later.

And then there was the whole succession thing. How was I supposed to feel about all this? Angry? Mad? Irritated? Humiliated? Or quietly chuffed that Dad thought I could follow in his footsteps … and scared witless for the same reason.

I felt all of the above, and more.

All in all, there was a lot for one tired, immensely sad, very confused and rather sleepy brain to take in, so that old sagging bed in our bedroom was never so welcome. Cordelia had made it up with fresh cotton sheets that were cool and soft to the touch. I stretched out and felt so clean and comfortable. It was good, even if my heart was breaking and my head was spinning with crazy possibilities.

I told Pippa what Mattie had said about my father and I cried and she cried and she comforted me. We held each other close she kissed me on the cheek before we went asleep. That kiss sealed something between us. Pippa and I have a special bond that nothing will break, no matter what happens in the future, or what I might become.

After that, I slept. After all I'd seen and heard, I shouldn't have got a wink of sleep, but I slept all night. Something to do with being in Sandybrook House, I reckon. If there's somewhere else on the planet that feels more like an oasis of pure peace, I'll eat my hat.

Mattie stayed the night in the room that Joshua, Damian and Thomas had shared earlier in the week. We woke early and Cordelia had our own clothes all washed and dried and ironed which made me wonder if that woman ever slept. Maybe the magic of Sandybrook didn't work for her in the same way it did for me. I took a bath and put on my clothes. I wanted Mattie to see the two holes in his sweater so he'd understand why I thought of it as my magic cloak.

Cordelia offered us fried eggs but I declined and took some toast. It was very quiet and calm in the kitchen. Mattie asked me to give his love to Mum and Dad. It was so mundane. I'd imagined bringing home these melodramatic missives from the anguished son:

Dear Father, I hate you for what you are doing and I will never support you or your policies. But I love you too. Your heartbroken son, Matthew.

OK, so it's bad soap opera but that's the point: instead of tearful histrionics I had to face the sad fact that we were a pretty normal family who loved each other. How boring is that?

The whole helicopter arriving and us departing routine was conducted with the minimum of fuss. Cordelia said goodbye and I promised I'd come back, to which she said, 'Of course you will, my dear.' And that was that.

Daisy and Mrs Devereux were nowhere to be seen. Mattie hugged me and said he'd see me soon. Then the soldiers who formed the cordon around the house made a guard of honour and Pippa and I got on the helicopter and we were up and away.

The best surprise of all was that Geraldine was on the helicopter and when I saw her I hugged her and she hugged me back and there was no hesitation on either side. Yes, things were looking up – though in fact I spent the short trip home looking down. The pilot pointed out landmarks. He didn't have to point out the Great River, which looked as vast as a sea in places. I thought about our poor old boatman and a tear escaped down my cheek.

And guess what? From the sky it was impossible to tell who was legal and who was illegal and where one zone finished and the next began. OK, that might seem like a trite and sentimental observation worthy of one of John's disciples to be followed by a hippy hymn, but tell me I'm wrong, if you can.

And before I knew it, the helicopter landed in the Citadel.

33

On the flight in the helicopter I'd been building up a head of steam about all the things Dad had kept from me and I was determined to show him that the trip he'd planned had worked in one important respect – I was not going to be kept in the dark any more about his ideas for me.

Yes, I, Valentina O'Connor, was returning with a whole new perspective on who controlled my life, So I was preparing a slightly frosty greeting to show Dad my obvious displeasure at having been taken for a fool. If he thought me presidential material – the idea was growing on me – he'd better start treating me like a human being with a fully functioning brain. And there was some serious talking to be done.

I stepped off the helicopter and saw Dad standing on his own on the roof of the Hrad, waiting for me, and I remembered what Mattie had told me about his illness (not that I'd exactly forgotten it) and all my pre-planning went out the window. There was my Dad and I was never so happy to see him. I ran and practically knocked him over in my eagerness to hug him and he hugged me back and I wasn't letting go and it was so good. Forget all that presidential stuff; I was Daddy's Little Girl and I decided that the new me could wait for another day.

Poor Pippa. Dad gave her a friendly handshake but it was more than a bit of an anticlimax after what we had endured. Pippa's family situation was definitely moving to the top of my new agenda of things to do and people to help.

Meeting Mum was a more subdued affair than my reunion with Dad. That's just the way things are between me and her, and when she asked me how I was, I almost said 'fine' but managed to hold it back.

'I've so much to tell you, Mum,' I said, and she beamed a smile at me that made me realise how easy it is to be nice to people, especially the people who love you.

'I'm so happy you're back, Valentina; so, so happy.'

'Me too, Mum.'

'When you get settled, I'll have Francesca bring us some tea and we'll talk.'

Francesca came in, then, and Bridget, who had prepared my favourite dinner. And when the welcome homes were completed (how much did they know about what had happened to me? Not much, I suspect, but I'm sure they sensed Mum and Dad's anxiety), I went to my room and closed the door. It was SO good to be back in my own space.

Eccles and I spent some quality time together, and I enjoyed being on my own for a bit, much as I love Pippa, who was given one of the guest suites.

I did silly things like open my wardrobe and touch my clothes and pick up my favourite shoes – though, to be honest, I was embarrassed by the quantities of shoes I owned. If I become president, I don't want to be remembered for my extravagant taste in shoes. (I once read an article on Imelda Marcos. Apart from all the real crimes she stands accused of, she committed some serious crimes against good taste – all that money and so many ugly shoes! Still, she serves as a warning to me.)

Later, we ate the dinner that Bridget had prepared. It was delicious. Dad was still working, which worried me. Shouldn't he be taking it easy?

'Where's Dad?' I asked, trying to sound casual.

'He'll be home soon,' Mum said and I knew by the way she looked at me that she knew that I knew. 'Don't worry,' she added.

Then she told me about Dad. The prognosis was uncertain. At the moment he was good, but there was no definite cure and the best that could be hoped for was that the doctors would manage his condition until there was a breakthrough in the treatment. There had been some promising results from a new drug developed in the Pilgrim medical research centre. She didn't sugar the news or pretend everything would be all right. Nor did she exaggerate or try to pass the worry onto me. She was clear and precise and calm. I knew she was saying, 'I know you can handle this, Valentina,' and I did. She didn't say anything about me becoming Dad's successor, and I didn't either.

The talk with Dad didn't take place for a few weeks. He made his illness sound like a head cold which might make life a little awkward for all of us. It would be a great source of comfort to him, he said, if he knew I was willing to give him a hand and learn the ropes in the 'family business', which is government. That's the way Dad introduced the whole succession issue. (I began to see what Mattie meant, about how alike we are, me and Dad.) Now we have frequent little chats and he forces me to think clearly. And, of course, I ply him with questions. I have so much to learn.

'There are no easy answers, Valentina,' Dad says. 'If we let everyone come to the island who wants to come, or if we open the borders of the Green Zone, we'll all perish. There's no two ways about it. The world is sinking and we're one small lifeboat. We do as much as we can, but if we try to save everyone, we'll all go down.' He pauses. 'I find the business of selling citizenship distasteful. But we use the money wisely.'

He smiles at me then.

'Think carefully about any changes you want to make and discuss your ideas with your mother and Joshua.'

That's the nearest he's come to saying 'after I die'.

34

A week after we returned from the Badlands and had been certified pure and free from all diseases and contagions, Pippa and I were back in school. Pippa's stock rose dramatically after she came to live with us during term time.

I never really fitted in, in school. I admit I've always felt a little removed from the whole school thing. So let's just say that the Badlands experience made me feel older than my years – in the way that Damian seemed older than me when I first met him. I mean, after what Pippa and I had been through, how could we possibly be interested in what the jocks and socks are up to in the locker room?

Speaking of which, Sarah Flicker and Jonathan Little continued as head boy and head girl for the remainder of the year – as I predicted – with no public consequences for their unbecoming behaviour in the boys' shower room. In fact, they became iconic figures whose fame lives on in Thomas Aquinas High School. Almost immediately after the incident, the toilet cubicle, where rumour now has it they went the whole way, became a revered place of secret pilgrimage for a small army of extremely silly and irritating girls who took their chastity rings off and pledged themselves to romantic love. And we all know how romantic a place a boys' toilet is! Nonetheless, the practice lives on.

There had been a complete news blackout on my adventure in the Badlands. As far as the state media was concerned, I was never there. But that didn't stop the rumours about the miracles (they'd increased and multiplied) I'd performed reaching the school: healing the sick, resurrecting the dead and changing water into wine (oh, God!). A whole bunch of junior girls (the ones who were not busy making an altar in the cubicle where Sarah and Jonathan had done 'it') were busy creating a cult dedicated to Princess Valentina, which was seriously embarrassing, irritating and tiresome, especially when one group began following me around the school. I generally ignored them but one day I acknowledged their presence and one girl fell into a swoon and the others started to scream and entered into a 'devotional frenzy' (that's a phrase I picked up in a book I read on cults) and the whole thing got seriously out of hand. Matron was not pleased and poor old Rumsfeld was seriously peed off but, hey, what could I do?

The sweeter side of the Valentina cult was that my devotees took to placing little gift offerings on my desk or beside my locker. The cult business lasted about a term before it (thankfully) petered out, but it still occasionally raises its head.

You're wondering about Damian. Well, he came back to school after Christmas. He was quieter and less sure of himself, so it was good that Thomas was there to act as his minder. Yes, I did say Thomas. And yes, I did arrange it. It's amazing how adept I've become at making reasoned arguments for good causes. What's the point of having influence if you don't use it to do some good? OK, call it patronage but it's enlightened patronage. I sound like Dad, I know. Can't be helped.

Me and Damian? We're good friends – best friends – but nothing else. Don't get me wrong; I love him, but not in that starry-eyed way I did when I first met him. In general, I don't think girls of my age should date boys of the same age. The emotional gap is too great. It's got nothing to do with being fickle. It's just the way things are.

Anyway, I've met someone – he works as a PA for the Minister of Climate Change Research and I'd describe him as 'hot' if it wasn't the worst pun in the world. He's a few years older than me, and he's going to escort me to the next state dinner (for a visiting delegation of Asian leaders). Joshua will accompany Pippa – surprise, surprise. I'm not sure I quite approve of that relationship – I think she's too young to be that serious, and I think he's too old to be interested in someone her age. Yes, I know she's smarter than anyone else of her age but she's still only a teenager. I'm not her mother, though, so she'll have to figure it out for herself.

So, has my life changed beyond all recognition? Am I mobbed in the streets? Does my poster adorn the bedroom walls of thousands of adoring fans? (I sincerely hope not.) In short, no. Things are much the same as they were before.

Incidentally, the Pilgrim community has gone international and John is now a serious megastar, so we do have one in the family, and that is quite enough.

The biggest change is in my head. I've seen a lot, I've learned a lot and I'm still watching and asking and learning and thinking and planning what I can do to help the people I met in the Badlands.

The second biggest change is that my room is now only cleaned once a week (Mum was fine but Francesca took a bit of persuading), and I put up whatever I like on the walls – like a detailed and proper map of the island. How exciting is that?

I did go back. Once to the Amber Zone to visit a quarantine centre and once to the Badlands. They were both 'private' visits. In other words, the council wanted nothing to do with it – bad precedent and all that stuff. That doesn't mean that there weren't a hundred hoops to jump through before I got the reluctant and begrudging go-ahead, not to mention the vaccinations and the periods of quarantine when I came back.

Poor Geraldine. She had to go through the whole rigmarole too. Neither visit was reported in the official media. I knew there was much tut-tutting and humming and hawing in the council about my first visit to the Amber Zone but that was nothing compared to the waves caused when I asked permission to attend the opening of a Solidarity-run hospital in Newtown on the Great River. Dad was at his most inscrutable, merely asking me why I wanted to go.

'To show the people who helped me that I haven't forgotten them,' I said.

Dad gave me one of his long hard looks but didn't say anything. Mum didn't say anything either; she didn't have to. But the point is they didn't stop me from going. They gave me scope to make my own decisions and be my own person. That was important to me.

I'd love to be able to say that the visit to the Badlands was a triumph and I felt totally vindicated. But I can't, because it wasn't. On the positive side, things have moved on in Newtown. There's a town council and a police force. And there were a million of our soldiers on duty so I didn't feel at risk or in harm's way. What I hadn't reckoned on was the size of the crowd that showed up to greet me at the hospital. I mean, it was massive. So many people that it was scary. So many people I am going to be responsible for.

Once inside, all the protocols that Dad's advisors had dreamed up for me went out the window. They wanted me to wear a face mask to prevent myself inhaling contaminated air, and I wasn't to have any physical contact with the patients. How likely was that? Once inside the door, I was mobbed by patients and staff and everyone wanted to touch my hand or hug me or even touch my clothes. But I managed to finish the tour in one piece and I made a little speech and accepted a bouquet of flowers and promised I'd be back.

The real panic occurred when I went outside. The crowd surged and there was a stampede. It was horrible. The police couldn't hold people back and the soldiers got jumpy and fired shots over the heads of the crowd. It was pandemonium. No one was killed but loads of people were injured. And, of course, the whole thing was reported in the illegal press, so you could say I put back the cause of unifying the island by a decade or so. (Yeah, it is a cause and I support it.) So much for making my own decisions. Mum and Dad didn't say anything. They didn't have to.

So, there you go. I'm getting ready to be president. I'm not exactly giddy with excitement, but neither am I frightened by the idea any more – I'm my father's daughter, after all. I think I know what people want. You don't have to be a genius to figure it out: they want to live in peace without feeling afraid; they want to have enough food, enough clothes and a warm place to live. And we've got to make this happen without destroying ourselves or the island in the process. Easy, peasy, eh?

I've grown up over the last two years. And I'm lucky. I'm surrounded by people who love me. That's important – really important. But it's lonely, too, sometimes, especially when I think that Dad might die soon and if (when) I succeed him I'll have power over life and death.

Death.

I have a nightmare from time to time. In it, all the bodies I saw in the Badlands come back to life. Or the boatman, Hakim's twin, the one who gave his life for me, comes and stands at the end of my bed and says, 'Don't let me down.' I hope I don't let him down, or all the people in the Badlands who look to me to help them.

So, that's my story.

Am I ready to become the president? No, of course not. It's been two years since all this happened, and I've got to do some more growing up in the meantime, but I'm still only sixteen. How could I be ready for that? But it may happen sooner rather than later. And if it does, I'll do what he's asked me to, and do it as well as I possibly can. Because that's who I am.

I'm Valentina O' Connor, the girl who will be president.

glossary

Amber Zone: Area under the influence of the State of Free Citizens, many of them from the Tribe. Population of 3 million.

AOT: Army of the Tribe – an armed group that wants to keep the island for the Tribe and which is opposed to the presence of immigrants on the island.

Badlands: The lands beyond the Great River, also known as the **Red Zone**. Lawless, highly populated and dangerous, with as many as ten million inhabitants, many of whom are climate refugees.

Book of Rules: The laws and customs of the State of Free Citizens. All families and individual citizens must abide by the rules.

Citadel: Most secure and exclusive area in the Green Zone. A multicultural community where wealth counts.

Council: The government of the State of Free Citizens.

Elite: One of three hundred families allowed to live in the Citadel. Each family may have up to twenty members, including parents, children, grandparents and grandchildren. When a woman marries within the Citadel, she is counted among her husband's family. If a member of a family is expecting a child which will bring the number of the family to more than twenty, the family must apply to the Council of State for permission to keep the child. Permission is normally granted on payment of a fee. When a vacancy arises in the Citadel, applicants must pay a fee to apply and a fee on acceptance. Yearly payments are also made. A family is expected to keep five servants.

Green Zone: The area under the full control of the Council of State with a population of 300,000.

Solidarity: Non-governmental group that assists illegal immigrants and opposes the AOT and the criminal gangs who prey on immigrants.

Specials: Anti-terrorist police based in the Hrad.

Tribe: The original settlers of the island.

Valley of the Thrushes: The valley where the Pilgrims have their community.